Law & Desire

by

Michael Allen Zell

Lavender Ink
New Orleans
lavenderink.org
ᜧ

Law & Desire
by Michael Allen Zell
Copyright © 2016 by Michael Allen Zell and Lavender Ink
Printed in the U.S.A.
First Printing
10 9 8 7 6 5 4 3 2 1   16 17 18 19 20 21
Cover Photo: Louis Maistros
Cover and Book design: Bill Lavender
Author Photo: Thom Bennett
Library of Congress Control Number: 2016935999
Zell, Michael.
Law & Desire / Michael Allen Zell
p. cm.
ISBN: 978-1-944884-05-5 (pbk.)

Law & Desire

In these city streets everywhere
You gotta be careful
Where you move your feet
How you part your hair.

—Curtis Mayfield

For Rebecca

Chapter 1

"What the hell you thinkin'?" snarled the car dealer at the phone. His nostrils flared.

He had a voice both smooth and sharp, like molasses stuck in the throat. His pudginess barely shimmered in the wake of his question, because the car dealer wasn't angry, only annoyed.

"It's Good Friday. We was wantin' twenty pounds crawfish tuh berl. I was hopin' for a li'l more paper. Two-nuh-half bills a day," said the runner.

He sounded like a limp handshake deluded it was a champion arm wrestler. Anything asked for would be denied by the other party based on nuisance factor alone.

The car dealer snorted in derision. "Gotdamn if you ain't gotta mouth on you. Deluded sense of self-worth. You ain't shit. I train any kid out there do your job. I'll tell you what else, speaking of crawfish," said the car dealer before pausing to wipe his nose.

Good Friday in New Orleans is a special day, even for those not religiously inclined. This is partly due to the fact that everyone in the city is de facto Catholic.

A person doesn't have to ever attend Mass or have the priest wipe ash on a penitent forehead to be bound by the calendar that makes life in the Crescent City unique. Anyone; black, white, brown, or otherwise need not be devout to have a Good Friday crawfish boil as tradition.

The car dealer continued. "Damn well better make sure get them deliveries to the frat houses, lawyer at his office, deputy mayor at his family's bar, and schoolteacher at his house 'fore you buy one pound-a crawfish. Them white mens don't like waiting. 'Specially regulars. Double-'specially they gotta deal with family shit this weekend. And shut your mouth 'bout more money. Two bills good pay for a day's work, boy."

"Yessir," was the chastened reply.

"Better not wear them socks again. You know what I'm talkin' 'bout."

Again, "Yessir," was the answer.

"May as well be wearin' a sign sayin' 'My dumb ass is holdin'. Frisk me,' you go out on a run wearin' them socks. Black socks with magenta weed leaves on 'em. Thought I didn't know the color, did you?" the car dealer asked.

"Guess what? I know colors. Don't matter whether all them pretty 7-pointed weed leaves are sienna, cerise, or magenta, 'cuz they shouldn't be on the socks of my runner. If I find out you wearin' 'em like a big sign, it's your ass."

He paused. "Be careful what you say. Tell me, 'But I'm the weed man,' right now like before, it's your ass. Hear me? I'll smack the carefree right off your face."

The runner replied, "Yessir," for the third time but not too indignantly. He was looking down at shorts so long and sagging so low that what with the socks pulled up high above his Adidas sandals, none of the ebony skin of his legs showed.

The socks were precisely the ones spoken of, though the runner had thought the color of pot leaves printed all over them was red. He did wear them for the reason he'd previously stated to his boss, the same reason thrown back in his face. Pride.

He *was* the weed man. Not one who waited on the street for business but one who delivered to customers, mostly of the white well-heeled type.

No way he was going to explain this rationale to his boss again, much less the additional pride that it also meant coke man and heroin man, naturally speedball man too, so he just denied.

"Alright," said the car dealer resignedly. He looked at the

phone in disgust and picked his nose. "Remember, hype the dope to the lawyer and schoolteacher. We been lacin' their weed with heroin 'bout two weeks, so they don't know they ready, but they ready. Let 'em know heroin's happenin' now. They can smoke it. No needles. Those mens don't want no needle marks. Hear me? I expect their next order gonna be dope."

The runner affirmed this, knowing his raise was off the table, and then listened briefly to the dial tone of an empty line. At that point, he sneered at the phone and said matter-of-factly, "I *am* the weed man."

The car dealer placed his phone on a table otherwise filled with dirty dishes. Wiped the index finger of his other hand on his Saints jersey. Hadn't been a little snot nose for decades, but his sinuses were always active.

"Gotdamn if you ain't gotta deal with people trying to keep you from succeeding, Leon Sparks," he said aloud. "Workin' your last nerve. Kid thinks he deserves $250 a day."

He walked over to his closed drapes and peeked outside. It was midday, and the weather was beautiful. Though Sparks was inside, he could just about smell the light breeze of spring.

The view afforded him the side of his neighbor's house and the stretch of street leading Jackson toward Magazine. The lakeside neighbor had a row of sweet olive trees around the entire façade of her house.

Leon Sparks, on the other hand, had a landscaper put in the scrubbiest little bushes around his place pocket change could buy. He wanted the mere semblance of typical domestic usualness. Didn't care to see if he had a green thumb, so why bother with planting anything else? Could just smell his neighbor's aromatic trees anyway.

The brown face that reflected in the window from between two slightly pulled-back curtains was lighter than the one he was born with. Monthly bleach cream for the past thirty years had done that.

As first a young assistant then eventually the boss at the West Bank car lot, he had ingrained the teachings of his first employer there to, "Get yourself as light as possible. Sell more cars that way. Even our black brothers and sisters have been brainwashed that bright is better."

Sparks lived alone on Jackson in the shotgun house he owned. Never had company. That was for the best.

The front parlor was filled with plastic milk crates stacked five high and ten across along musty carpet. Junk stuffed the crates. Umpteen Crown Royal bottles with their purple velvet bags stood throughout the entire first floor against walls, on counters, and any other available surface. The walls were filled with magazine pictures of women in lewd poses. The images were framed by stapling them to alternating black and red construction paper of three different sizes.

His second floor was worse.

Sparks simply lived how he lived. There was no incongruity to that, at least in his own mind. Silence is deafening to many who live alone, so they use the sound of radio or television to counteract. Sparks used his noisy décor.

Things got interesting in regards to his hustle, which was directly connected to his job. In addition to selling the expected wares through A+ Used Cars in Harvey along the West Bank Expressway, Sparks augmented his income, if the term "augment" can mean making exponentially more money off the books than his W-2 income yielded.

His bleach cream advocating boss was the straight-laced sort, but when Sparks took over A+, he knew there had to be another angle. It showed itself by way of disaster.

While Sparks was evacuated in Houston during the Hurricane Katrina-induced levee failures, he met a man with a proposition. Gas station franchise owner was the official title, but his hustle was importing drugs from Mexico and South America. So much that he needed more buyers, particularly in the New Orleans market.

"Cut it, but don't be an asshole. There's plenty of money to make. You give a customer weak product, they go somewhere else," he'd instructed Sparks.

By 2006, business was booming at the little three-person office of A+ Used Cars. Many needed replacements for flooded-out cars, so sales were up.

Sparks had replaced his assistant with a mechanic who would keep his mouth shut. For additional pay, A+'s longtime office manager was on board.

Sparks had purchased a simple 2-car trailer that only he pulled by pickup truck at least once a month to Houston. The panels of the cars served as shells for storage of the payment made for drugs that were transported the six hour drive back to Harvey, across the river from New Orleans.

He made sure he had enough drug mule cars, so a few easy sales were turned down. It went against his grain to some extent, but he learned quickly that the bird in the hand paled in comparison to ten in the bush.

The next phone call Leon Sparks received on Good Friday was quite different than the first. It may not defy belief that for several years the only female companionship Sparks had came with an hourly charge.

A+ was closed for the holiday, and Sparks had all calls redirected to his personal line. He wasn't paying close enough attention to notice that the one received shortly after his dinner was such a call.

"Yeah," he answered with a slouch that came from having fallen asleep on the couch for hours.

The reply was with a tone that would've brought him to life even if she was reciting the alphabet.

"Hey, baby. I'm trying to reach Mr. Leon Sparks. You him? Sounds like it," she purred.

"Who might this be?" was his curiosity-piqued response.

"This *is* you, Leon. I knew it. Ooh, honey, it's good to hear your voice. I've been thinkin' about it ever since our time together."

Sparks was on the verge of picking his nose again, but his index finger stayed frozen in the air.

"Wait a minute? Who is this?" he asked, still a little skeptical.

"It's Vanessa Davis, silly. Remember me? Creole from Opelousas. I was in New Orleans a little while back. I don't mind telling you, Leon, we were so good together I've been craving it."

Sparks raised his eyebrows, and his nostrils flared. He tried desperately to remember her. "What did you say your name was, ma'am?" he questioned in his most polite way.

"Vanessa Davis. Now honey, shame on you if you don't remember me. How you gonna do me like that?"

Not waiting for Sparks to reply, she spoke to others in the room with her.

"Well, girls. He doesn't remember. Gave it to me like he'd been locked up for a decade. Wasn't gonna charge him this time it was so good. Guess you three are out of luck too."

Sparks heard a few disappointed voices, one of them protesting with, "Thought you said he'd be up for it. I really need that D."

Sparks was worried Vanessa was about to hang up. He blurted out, "Wait. What did you have in mind?"

"Leon, don't make me beg," was the pleading that drove away any remaining skepticism while also shifting his sense of reason from the grey matter above to the blood vessels below.

She followed that with, "Some friends of mine are in town for the weekend. All pretty Creole country girls just like me.

Leon, we each want a man. After I told them about you, we all want the same man."

Sparks' so-called sense of reason was now at half-mast.

"I think that sounds real good," he stammered. Watching what he said so as not to ruin a sure thing, he said, "So, uh, where can we all meet?"

"Leon, you do remember me," she said. "Come to Capri Motel on Tulane Avenue in an hour. Room 138. We just checked in."

Dreaming of a beast with many backs, Leon looked at his clock to see it was 7:12 p.m.

By the time she hung up, he was halfway across the room to take a shower and try to locate his suavest clothing. He initially put on a clean Saints jersey but thought better of it and found a button-up shirt.

The four women on the other end of the line were more subdued. They all had three things in common. The first, unknown by each about the other, was that all four of them felt defined by the skin of their torsos.

The one who called Leon Sparks had a tattoo running vertically from the underside of her left breast straight down to above her hip that read in cursive, "Excuse me while I kiss the sky."

The one who called out about needing it right now had bruises throughout her chest from a man who'd beaten her for years.

Of the other two, one had stretch marks from two births, and the other had scar tissue along the right of her stomach from a childhood bicycle accident.

Only the first of the four was neither embarrassed nor ashamed of her markings and didn't try to cover them even when intimate, but she along with the others had another thing in common.

None of them were meeting Leon Sparks because they wanted to. It was either that or be registered as sex offenders for the rest of their lives. They were being leveraged.

If it was Sparks or them, then it was going to be Sparks. One of them stated that in so many words after the phone call. None of the four were in a very good mood when the call ended, but they knew their job was halfway done.

The others in the motel room told them so.

Across the city, before the big date of Leon Sparks, thousands ate boiled crawfish. Five to thirty gallon pots were also filled with corn, potatoes, and a mix of enough spices to tingle the lips of the eaters once all the food was poured out onto newspaper covered tables.

A few in the French Quarter were doing the same thing less communally in restaurants while paying two to three times as much per pound as those outside the historic area.

In fact, while Sparks prepared himself, many in the Quarter were struck by sights of the type not seen at home.

A few amateur photographers documented several items, in particular the new solar powered trash cans recently added to tourist-district streets. The odd juxtaposition of $3,000 receptacles on sidewalks adjacent to non-working streetlights and roads full of axle-breaking potholes was not lost on many, even though most didn't know the price tag or that several of the trash cans didn't work.

This was New Orleans summed up. Broken cookies in a brand new bag, provided someone politically-connected was profiting from the sale.

Another hit of the point-and-click crowd was Metairie activist Morris Grange. Louisiana had been dubbed Hollywood South due to all the movie productions resulting from generous state-offered tax credits.

Grange figured with enough folk around he could make his

newest aggrievement public in Jackson Square. He was on his own, as his usual followers were confused by his parting from the typical course of telling everyone, including the religious, they were damned.

"End Whitesploitation!" read his sloppily-written sign. The only prop since the large cross with scrolling LED display had been left at home.

Grange's bullhorn-amplified voice carried throughout the public square. "Stop watching Hollywood movies. They're bad for us. None of 'em do anything but make white people look childish, silly, less than human. It's exploitation. Whitesploitation!" he exclaimed.

While a few trash cans compacted trash, and Grange, on the other hand, released debris into the world, Leon Sparks was driving from Uptown to his destination of desire.

"A lucky man right here!" Sparks yelled at the inside of his car. He'd taken a pill that promised he'd be going for hours. He was so revved up and in the mood for action that he had no doubt what was about to happen.

It was a bareback night for him. No protection on hand. No gun. No rubber. "Gonna rawdog tonight," he said.

After taking his usual way, he passed condos, restaurants, and bars on Tulane, many of them only days or months old, in the few blocks before the motel's sign beckoned on the left. "Motel" was lit in large vertical letters, while "Capri" looked an afterthought at the bottom.

Nightfall had come later what with the arrival of spring and daylight savings time. When Sparks pulled into the parking lot, with the large brick Dixie Brewing building at his back, he saw the car's clock read 8:15.

Room 138 was located on the first floor at the far end of the left hand side. Sparks slowly eased past the office to an empty parking spot near the room. He hadn't used the particular room in the past but knew which one it was.

Sparks checked himself in the rear-view mirror and ambled to the door in front of his car. There were only a few vehicles in the lot since it was still early for the type of clientele the hotel generally hosted.

Thin tan curtains were closed. Light glowed through them. Sparks turned his ear toward the door and heard a few female voices casually talking. He took a deep breath, sniffed, and smiled broadly as he knocked twice on the door.

The voice he recognized from the phone called out, "Who is it?"

He tried to keep his obvious anticipation at bay when answering, "Leon. Leon Sparks ready to party."

When he stepped through the opened door shortly after, beckoned by only a curling finger and sultry, "Come in, honey," Sparks' excitement first turned to confusion.

Three women were silently standing on the far side of the bed and turned so he couldn't make out their faces. He quickly looked behind the door to see two masked men who both reached out and Tased him.

While he was sprawled on his stomach, Sparks felt the tightening of cuffs on his wrists and ankles. He sensed even more men in the room.

His first point of focus was hearing a much harsher version of the phone voice say, "I did my part. Acted like a fucking rat. My record stays clean. You hear me? Turnin' tricks won't make me no sex offender."

The other women assented, but all of them quickly scurried out of the room when Leon Sparks craned his neck to get a view of them. He saw enough to know they weren't pretty Creole darlings just in from the country.

None of the four women would make it through the thorny days of physical harm by men or self-abuse by drugs to see

2016.

"Gotdamn if I ain't been catfished by some dirty bitches," Sparks fumed as he floundered on his belly.

"Looks like you're the bitch, Leon," mocked one of the two men who lifted him up by his arms.

Before Sparks could reply, his head jerked back by a piece of material tossed over his head from behind and yanked painfully tight in and across his mouth as a gag. That was followed by a hood covering his head.

The material felt like nylon. It smelled like the sweat, fear, and desperation of those who'd previously worn it.

Sparks was roughly led out of the room. Heard a car door open before he was shoved forward. He put his hands out to keep from going face-first. The material that banged up his knuckles and arms was metal. Felt like a van.

The door closed behind him.

"What the hell you thinkin', Leon?" Sparks said aloud, sounding with the gag on like his wisdom teeth had just been pulled, and jumping seconds later from a cough less than five feet away.

"You don't have to do this," Sparks pleaded. "How much you want to open that door and let me out?"

"Shut the fuck up," was the reply. Sparks suspected the voice, unlike those of the men he'd heard inside the motel room, was that of a black man.

"Brother, please. Name your price," Sparks tried, though it came out like, "Bwuhwuh, pwee. Nay yuh pwy."

He was met with silence, as were the rest of his tries over the following seventeen minutes. But while he pled aloud, his mind was actively counting and sensing the motion of the van.

Sparks was next able to see and speak when, after the vehicle stopped, he was pulled into a building. His hood and gag were removed.

He looked around to find he was inside a blighted space.

While he continued to scan the large room, he saw at least twenty metal cells, each big enough to hold a sitting man and little more. With his senses more engaged, he realized that most of the cages held an occupant. They were quiet, other than some muffled sounds that probably meant gags.

The six men facing the chair Sparks was seated in all had on masks of some sort. Only their eyes showed.

"C'mon, man. What the hell's this?" Sparks asserted.

The man standing in front of the others was wearing a suit and tie, as compared to the array of black cargo pants and long-sleeve shirts the other five sported.

"Leon, Leon," suit-and-tie said. "Sorry to bring you in like this, but we needed to meet. You wouldn't have come any other way. Am I wrong?"

Sparks noticed that a few of the caged prisoners moved forward to observe the interaction.

"You gonna put me in a cage?" Sparks asked, gesturing around with his head and eyes. "What I do to you?"

"That depends on you, Leon," the man said. "Here's the deal. We're going to be business partners one way or the other."

As the man spoke, Sparks further deciphered the accent. A car dealer heard all kinds. This one sounded born-and-raised here but college educated somewhere else.

"What you want with a rinky dink car lot?" Sparks tried.

The man laughed. "Leon, let's cut the b.s. The drugs, okay. We know what you're into. We're interested in a little piece."

"Hell, no," Sparks said resolutely.

"The thing is, you're only in a position to say yes," the man said. "25% yes. Or you go in a cage right now, and we talk again in a week."

Sparks again eyeballed his surroundings. The stairs to the second floor. The faded and peeling pink and blue paint. The rubble around him.

He thought about how much he was pulling in weekly. "This some bullshit," he rumbled.

In matter-of-fact fashion, the man replied, "No, it's simple. You agree now, you agree after spending time in a cage, or you don't leave this room alive."

Sparks spoke with anger but the throttled sort, "You kill me you get 25% of nothin'."

"That's true, of course, but do you really want to die today? You have years in front of you, Leon."

There was a pause while Sparks raised his cuffed hands to wipe his nose.

"Nah, I'm not goin' out like that," Sparks muttered. "How we work this out?"

The man spoke encouragingly. "There you go. Compliance, the wisest choice. Leon, truth be told, we like you. Not one of the violent types. Businessman as a front. That said, we can get to you anytime we want. Don't forget it's to your benefit to keep us happy. Now, details."

About three-quarters of an hour later, Leon Sparks was again gagged and hooded, reversing the trip back to the motel. He was promptly pistol-whipped after being pulled inside. When he came to in the room where his nightmare began, his hand and ankles were no longer cuffed.

Chapter 2

Bobby Delery was on his back, prone but not motionless. He was using the breathing learned in Tai Chi class. In through the nostrils while the lower belly expanded. Out through the mouth while the arc receded. Tongue touching the roof of the mouth behind the teeth. A quicker alternating count than the longer slower version Sifu Aaron, his teacher, had taught.

His brow was sweaty, and his muscles were on edge. He looked up at Ellis Smith. She was glistening, not working harder than him, but differently. Ellis rose up and down. Back was ruler-straight. Legs folded beneath her. She clenched her teeth. Her hair was pulled back into a ponytail.

Delery saw her straining. Ellis' natural beauty warmed him. He wasn't speculating with the quick thought, "Don't need makeup. You look good when you wake up." They'd been meeting for this three times a week going on two months. Both had taken the day off.

He could tell she'd almost pushed herself to the limit. So had he. Delery exerted three more times from the waist down, thighs tensing, feet flexing.

They both finished at the same time. Bodies relaxed from the exertion. Action ceased for a few seconds.

Delery loudly huffed to make aloud his feeling of exhausted completion. He sat up and pulled himself off of the leg press machine. Three-quarters of the iron stack. Three sets of fifteen reps. Same number of sets and reps he did on the other machines. Legs today.

Ellis was catching her breath and shaking her arms to loosen up.

"Ten of 'em," she said.

He nodded. She'd been doing dips, sinking down and pulling back up with arm strength. It was unusual for them to finish their half-hour workouts at precisely the same time, much less to be using adjacent pieces of equipment.

They'd been dating for going on nine months, ever since meeting by happenstance at the bookshop on Chartres. He was 43, and she found dating was typically more traditional with him than those closer to her age of 29.

Delery and Ellis got on well and enjoyed each other's company. Neither dared utter the "L word" aloud though both had increasingly thought it.

As they left the gym, he whispered, "It's still Friday morning. Want another workout?"

She raised a chiding but flirtatious eyebrow. "I'm sweaty."

"Yes you are. Even better. You're a fine, fine woman," he said.

"Mmm hmm," she said. "What do you think that flattery's gonna get you?"

"A real good place in about ten minutes," Delery replied, tired but with anticipation.

Ellis smiled knowingly, breaking her faux lack of interest. She nodded, speaking only with her brown eyes, saying, "Yes, it sure will, and I'm looking forward to it as much as you are."

A shared hour, shower, and lunch later, he asked, "Wanna take a walk with me over to Euclid, see what new records they have?"

"I think I'll stay here and read."

Delery looked over at her while walking to his shoes.

"Probably be a little bit."

Ellis smiled contentedly.

"Okay, Bobby. I'm gonna curl up on your couch," she said.

A brief walk on Dauphine took him past two junk shops and a few restaurants, a couple trendy and an equal number likely more durable. He turned on Piety toward the river and walked past Markey Park that few used, all the way to the end of the street.

Across Chartres, the metal bridge arched over the levee and train tracks to a fairly new park that ran alongside the Mississippi River. The bridge was dubbed the Rusty Rainbow, but the pot 'o gold Delery sought was on the neighborhood side.

Euclid Records was his blessing and curse. Living close to a two-story shop with good selection continually arriving. Deciding what *not* to buy was the problem, especially with all the reissues flooding the market.

Delery stepped up and into the shop, saw the manager was busy with a guy selling a stack of vinyl, and took the stairs on the right to the second floor where he liked to hit the Jazz and Soundtracks sections.

He grinned, remembering the events of the morning and the first real record store he'd ever been in. Tall Man One Stop on Pontiac Street in downtown Fort Wayne at a time the Indiana city was changing from the City of Churches to the City of Crack Houses. Pontiac had its share of both.

Tall Man was where Delery first heard Run DMC, Egyptian Lover, Mantronix, Kurtis Blow, Whodini and many others in the 80's. He'd failed at the first and only element of hip hop he tried, flopping around like a fool on a stray piece of cardboard, and had firmly decided to just enjoy the music.

His now-deceased father George was as confused by rap as he was twelve-year-old Delery attempting to spin around while scissoring legs.

"Bobby, what in the world is this?"

"Dad, I'm trying to breakdance."

Understandably mistaken that his son's inept flailing was actually how breakdancing was supposed to be done, George Delery had said, "That's not dancing. Looks like a worm, but what I'm talking about is this racket you're playing."

"You know what I think about listening to cassettes. Degrades your ears. And all I hear playing is drum machine racket. Sounds like your video games. How can you want to listen to this after hearing my James Brown records?"

Mind back on present day, Delery barely began through the New Arrivals before coming across a record by Phil Cohran.

He laughed out loud. "Well, how about that?"

Delery remembered the name as that of an older man he'd once seen play an amplified kalimba at Ethiopian Diamond, a restaurant up north on Broadway in Chicago. According to the sticker on the shrinkwrap, Cohran had played with eccentric jazz legend Sun Ra.

Delery thought, "It figures. Here I was feeling centered after this morning. Digging for vinyl, and I find a record that completes my timeline. New Orleans to Fort Wayne to Chicago, and now back home."

He trotted back downstairs like a parade pony, eager to pay and listen to the record with Ellis.

His found sound, equilibrium, and sense of all well was about to go south.

Delery came up on the finalization of the process he'd initially witnessed. It was an old story, repeated in every continent past and present. The haggle, the wiggle, the often adversarial jiggle. How much would a merchant pay a person for used items to resell?

The black man standing at the counter was tall and solid. His expensive track suit couldn't hide an emerging belly, and he sported crisp Jordans with laces tied. Looked like his head was probably shaved due to a receding hairline. He was at that age. A native, based on his accent.

By contrast, the manager David was a thin white man with a head of longish hair. He was wearing faded blue jeans, well-worn Chuck Taylors, and a frayed plaid shirt with mother-of-pearl buttons.

"Sorry, I can only do $35," he said, his voice of more recent New Orleans vintage.

"How about $40? A couple of these have gatefolds," was the reply.

"$35's a fair price. They're good records but not too uncommon."

Delery saw the man in front of him pause and tap his right index finger on his cheek. The delay seemed more the appearance of thought rather than considered thought.

"Alright. I guess I can live with that. A better deal next time, though."

While David opened the cash register, he was savvy enough to let the attempt at one-upmanship stand.

"Thanks for stoppin' in. What's your name? I'm David."

"My name's L.G. People call me Tiny."

Delery didn't hear David's reply while stepping off to the side to better assess Tiny. Could it be him after all these years? Hard to gauge if a child last seen at kindergarten age was the man before him. But he was called Tiny then. L.G. could be Lamar Gasper.

The man turned and left as Delery quickly paid for his record. By the time he briskly walked outside, the big guy was getting into a vehicle large enough to accommodate him.

Delery trotted over just as Tiny was about to close the door.

"Excuse me. Can I ask you a question?"

The larger man held tight to the door handle and squinted. "Who's asking?" sounded like it was muffled by burlap.

Delery stayed a couple steps from the vehicle. "You aren't Lamar Gasper, are you?"

Tiny eased the door closed a bit. "Like I said, who's asking?" A little sharper this time.

"My name's Bobby Delery. If you're Lamar and still go by Tiny, then you were probably my little brother Isaac's friend as a kid."

Tiny's mouth dropped, and he let go of the door handle. "No shit," barely stumbled out of his mouth.

The astonishment quickly turned to sadness.

"Friend as a kid? Been knowing him… Man, Isaac Delery was my boy 'til the day he died 'bout a year ago. He was a good man. They got him. That's real talk. You're his white looking older brother? I'll be. Kids used to call you Casper the Ghost, right?"

Now it was Delery's turned to be shocked, minus speech.

Tiny continued. "I didn't like that. You were Isaac's brother. Black like him, though you still don't look it. Plus, Casper sounds like Gasper. Really didn't like that. I think that's why I started going by Tiny."

"You knew my brother up 'til recently? Where was he living? What happened to him?" Delery asked. He ended the flurry of questions. "My dad said they all moved out of New Orleans years ago." His voice sounded like it rattled in his throat.

Tiny shook his head. His eyes glistened. He took a deep breath and paused.

"You're really Bobby Delery, huh? You need to prove that."

"Who else would I be? Why would I come up to you asking all this if I wasn't who I said I was?" Delery asked.

Tiny looked suspiciously all around them.

"C'mon, man. Show me some ID or I'm outta here," he said.

Delery stepped forward, took his driver's license out of his wallet, and showed it to Tiny.

Tiny looked at him with disgust. "Louisiana license and you live close. Here all this time and nobody knew it."

The fog continued to overtake Delery's mind. "I just got back last summer. Been living in Chicago. Do you know how to get ahold of my brother Curtis and my mama?"

Tiny's face showed the expression of a man who had to spill unfortunate truths. Terrible ones.

"Bobby, huh? Damn." He looked down and tapped the door. "Damn."

Before Delery could reply, Tiny sighed and said, "Come around and get up in the truck. You're not gonna like this, but you gotta hear it. We're gonna need a drink too. Let's go over to this place I like. Good people there."

After Delery called Ellis to let her know he'd be longer than expected and vaguely reassured her once she heard his tone, Tiny punctuated the short drive with the occasional head shake and a variation of "Bobby Delery back home" or "Damn, Bobby."

Tiny took Chartres and then North Peters along the levee, followed Elysian Fields up to St Claude, and made an illegal left turn. After bumping and thumping through a few blocks of streetcar construction, he veered off, turning right on St. Bernard. He followed the recently repaved and bike-laned street up to just before Urquhart and pulled next to a modest single story brick building.

A once-bright hand-painted sign attached to the building read "Lulu & Lonnie's." A piece of white poster board fastened to the closed door had three statements written in marker.

"No one under 25."

"No drugs."

"No cat selling."

Tiny and Delery went inside to hear Maze playing softly while a handful of black men held court at the bar. After greeting the bartender James and the small group, Tiny introduced Delery as his friend. He didn't use Delery's name and steered the other man to a table in the far corner after ordering a set-up.

"Sit quietly for a minute 'til James comes with the drinks. Good people here, but I can't take a chance," Tiny said firmly.

Delery wondered what he'd gotten himself into but realized he could easily get up and leave if necessary. He went back to Tai Chi breathing to try and calm himself.

After a couple minutes, their order arrived. A pint of Hennessy. Two cans of Coke. A bowl of ice cubes. Two glasses.

Delery followed Tiny's lead.

"They got him, Bobby. Janae and the kids too. Curtis got done the same night. That would've been easier, though," Tiny said.

With piercing eyes, he accused Delery, "It's none of my business 'bout family matters, but still. I know your parents split up. I don't understand, though. Your people. Why not get in touch all these years? It hurt Isaac. Probably Curtis too, underneath the façade. They didn't have your address or phone number. You must've remembered where you lived in New Orleans."

"I don't know what to say," Delery replied. "I sent them letters as a kid, but they never responded. My dad said they moved away a few years after that." His voice sounded like it came from his stomach.

"Whew," Tiny said. "As a li'l kid, Isaac heard your mama crying a few times and praying because you didn't get in touch. Again, none of my business, but I think you need a serious talk with your pops."

"He's dead," Bobby said. "Do you know how to get ahold of my mama?"

"Cancer got her. Must've been over twenty years ago. Curtis was living in the house after that, but he was a mess. Sorry to say it, a dope fiend. Burnt your mama's house down, him bein' on the pipe."

Delery took another sip. He'd been by the family home,

or rather the weed-filled lot with only the stoop remaining, a couple times since being stunned by the sight shortly after returning to New Orleans. The velocity of information was taking him in its wing and smothering. Not to mention that his dad must've been lying all those years.

"Sorry I'm the messenger of all this, but it was real hard for your mama after your pops and you left. She got by. We all do, right? Isaac rolled with it. Your baby brother Curtis was always gettin' in trouble," said Tiny.

"What happened to him? And Isaac?" asked Delery. His voice sounded like it came from his waist.

"That's why we're here," said Tiny. "A few days before it happened your brother was acting strange. He'd met with Curtis, trying again to get him to clean up. Something Isaac heard spooked him. Wouldn't talk about it."

"He didn't say anything?"

Tiny closed his eyes and shook his head.

"Shoot, it must've been something big. Isaac Delery didn't rattle. I guess you didn't know him, but he was real. Good man. Good father. Kinda guy who didn't have enemies."

For the first time since the record store, Delery's cognitive skills weren't muted, although his voice was.

"Isaac got killed for what he knew. You were his best friend. If somebody was willing to take out his whole family..." Delery paused.

"Right, right," Tiny said. "I don't know a thing, but if somebody thinks I do, then they might still want me quiet."

Delery poured more liquor and Coke into his glass and took a long sip to put it all down.

"Tiny, tell it to me straight," he said. "How'd they get killed? And don't worry about me. I haven't been back long, but if I ask anyone else about this, your name won't come up."

Tiny pulled a cigarette and lighter out of his pocket. "They say smoking's gonna be illegal in bars real soon. How about that? Man can't smoke in a bar."

He lit it and took close to five minutes to smoke while Delery waited silently.

"Isaac had a real pretty ride. Washed it every Saturday." Tiny paused. "Surprised you didn't hear about this up in Chicago. Thought it made the national news. Isaac, Janae, and Keira—she was their youngest—went to Andre's football game. It was a Friday night. St. Aug won. That was part of the news story. They must've all been coming home on Broad Street after the game. Andre too."

"There was a collision?" Delery asked softly. His voice sounded even further away, like it came all the way from his leg.

"No. Not a collision. No witnesses. Around 10:00, 10:30, people driving on Broad come up on a car not moving, a little bit back from the light at Bayou Road. They call it in, thinking it's a wreck, not seeing anybody. Cops show up expecting an abandoned vehicle. Maybe stolen for a joyride."

Tiny looked at an undefined spot in space. "Turns out it's Isaac's car all shot up from the front. Lousy motherfuckers killed that whole family. Even the kids. All of 'em took fire and were dead flat on their seats. Couldn't do an open casket for the funeral."

He looked back at Delery. Both saw the palpable pain in the eyes of the other man.

Both knew that in a bloody city like New Orleans no one stayed completely immune from and unaffected by violence, particularly if you were black. They knew this intellectually, but statistics and hypotheticals were useless when faced with grief that hollows you out and brings you to your knees.

"There's gotta be something you know that'll help me catch who did this. Wait, did NOPD collar anyone?" Delery asked.

"Nah, I checked with a friend of mine on the force, but it's a cold case. Something could turn up, change things, but right now…" Tiny sighed.

"Tiny, look. I'm a criminologist. That's my job. I can look into this," Delery said.

"Bobby, man, I appreciate you. I really do. But it's some street shit. You can't come here as an outsider. I know you're not, but you can't come here where people don't know you. Nobody's gonna talk."

Tiny poured the remaining cognac into each of their glasses, and they both finished off their drinks.

Delery pushed. "Tiny, this is my family. I gotta make it right. Can't you give me something that might help?" His voice was so faint it sounded like it came from below his foot.

Tiny narrowed his eyes and thought for a moment.

"You serious?" he asked.

"Definitely," Delery said. "Listen, I'm not gonna go all guns blazing on somebody, but I want justice," he emphasized, trying to regain strength. "You gotta tell me about how it happened to Curtis too."

Tiny gave in like he knew he eventually would.

"Course you do. I'm gonna give you an address. Tell him I sent you. It's cool you use my name. B might be able to take this on. I call him B, but to most people he's just Brotherman."

"Brotherman?" asked Delery. "Isn't everybody?"

Tiny revealed a knowing smile. "Everybody, uh huh, but this dude, he's *the* Brotherman."

Chapter 3

In October of 1953 Burl Grange fled the law and the brothers of his child-bride Jean to leave St. Louis for the woody Northshore of Louisiana, across Lake Pontchartrain from New Orleans. Eventually his fightin' and fussin', robbin' and cussin' put him in the ground.

Son Wilford, born six months after the move, spent his adult days in illegal gambling along with assorted petty frauds and schemes before returning from prison and retiring in the family house that no longer had the privacy of decades prior.

Now these are the names of the children of Wilford and Mary Grange.

Coleen, Celine, Matthew, and Morris.

To the casual bystander the children of Wilford were cut from a different cloth than him and their grandfather; however, the Grange offspring were a crafty lot who, much like a gecko changing colors to elude potential adversaries, naturally intuited a respectable public hue and an altogether different private pigment.

Their overconfidence in Grange evolution caused corruption and cynicism to multiply and grow in each of their souls.

And so it was most of all with the youngest, Morris.

Monstrously crippled in this way, he was like two men.

Most knew him as the leader of New Hope Men's Group, which was little more than a pseudo-religious twelve step program. His followers, simple-minded as they were, found him dynamic.

Those who weren't under his sway thought he sounded like a demented sheep with the opinions to match. It's true his voice held both the confidence, even arrogance, that ignorance breeds, and was filled with enough vibrato to trigger a seizure in a person with a weak nervous system.

Grange's complexion was that of a parched peach. Though he always appeared clean cut, the five 'o clock shadow of his soul threatened to unearth and reveal him as he was.

For the time being, both the hecklers unable or unwilling to understand his keen social commentary and the brass band loudly dusting off New Orleans' standards were enough to compel Grange to give up and leave Jackson Square with his bullhorn and whitesploitation sign. He'd put in his time for Good Friday.

Onlookers thought he looked dejected, but Grange was simply born with a downcast mouth. Several were correct, however, in their collective summation that he had no idea he was a cliché.

To be more precise, he was a walking cliché on his way back to the parking garage on Dauphine. He strode through the lovely weather with no hitch of disappointment in his step, only a pious sense of martyrdom.

Along the way up St. Peter the two blocks that took him past Royal and to Bourbon, Grange came upon an off-key busking couple, various conference attendees wearing their lanyards, the NOFD hanging a banner across the street for a spring festival, and a man carrying a woman and a snake down the sidewalk.

Grange had barely turned left onto Bourbon before he saw dueling signs of a different type than his own. An elderly white man wearing a camouflage cap and cowboy boots gestured his "Hairitage not hate" Confederate flag sign at a young black woman rocking camouflage shorts and cowboy boots who shook her "Black Lives Mattor" sign in response. One movement whose time had come and the other whose had passed.

U.S. history is a long series of people dragged kicking and

screaming into the future. The scene on Bourbon Street was one little link.

While they revisited an old story with the all too common Southern rigor of spelling, the two grammatically correct signs Grange viewed were on the wings. A vagrant spilled across the sidewalk on the left was passed out under his "Will Sex You For Food" scrawled on cardboard.

The barker standing upright on the other side tried the opposite tactic of thrusting the professionally printed "Big Ass Beers!" sign upward, around, and in the path of passersby like a freshman desperate to make it in the color guard.

"I've got something to say too," bleated Grange. He was tempted to join the fray, but a craving kept him moving through the wash of people along the busy street.

He passed hustlers of all types. The one-trick ponies who still played the "Bet you $5 I can tell you where you got them shoes" trick on tourists who were both astonished and delighted that the answer was "On your feet." The vagrants who draped cheap beads over necks before demanding tips. The older men who worked a little harder by selling free maps and directions to willing dupes. The dealers and hookers too. The racial disparity between hustlers and marks was literally black and white in most cases.

Regarding the next group of hustlers, it's said that the easiest place to hide is often right out in the open. This is especially the case if it's in the midst of those who are either unable or unwilling to see, much less those with no concern of its existence.

The latter in this case includes the city of New Orleans, NOPD, Bourbon Street business owners, and countless others. The former were the unknowing multitudes.

As Grange walked to cross Conti, three grade school-aged children tap danced next to a tip box. They looked to have little more to their names than the clothes on their backs.

A scowling guy called TJ stood about five feet from them. He always chose that spot or one directly across the street to wait. TJ, a child himself, who would've been in high school if he hadn't dropped out, wasn't observing so he could ensure huge tips.

He had prominent teeth and small gums, the type of person who typically only smiles as a matter of rare course, as not to reveal his mouth. In TJ's case, though, he'd stopped smiling when he was the same age as the boys clapping their hands and tapping the sidewalk with the bottle caps attached to their shoes.

He'd been one of them. Now he was in charge of them.

Grange's mind didn't compute when he saw a dinosaur-shaped man approach TJ. The pea-sized head, long leaning neck, voluminous figure, and loping stroll didn't make Grange think of a brontosaurus.

Grange also thought nothing out of the ordinary when he saw the dinosaur-man talk into TJ's ear and TJ responded in kind. When the two turned their backs to the street and the dinosaur-man plunged one of his short arms down so he could reach into his pocket and hand a few twenties to TJ, Grange only thought of himself and warbled, "It's time for an 8-ball."

Grange wasn't stunned to see TJ walk over to a tap dancer no older than ten and grab him roughly by the left arm to pull the little one to him. There was no concern when the child resisted and TJ backhanded him to the ear and right side of the face. No curiosity when TJ knelt down to the crying boy, blew into his nostrils, and said, "Listen, Peanut. Don't forget I'm God to you. I give you life or take it."

As Grange tapped his sign and bullhorn on separate hips, nothing out of the ordinary registered when he saw the child nod in affirmation, wipe tears away, stumble over to the dinosaur-man, and the two walked around the corner of Conti toward Rampart.

Grange continued on Bourbon until turning right on Bienville. Midway along the block he saw an evening swarm. They weren't bats, crows, pimps, or hoes, but bicyclists.

Seven of them angrily surrounded a feisty man wearing a fake beard and tall drum major hat. In addition to his get-up, he sat on a cheap bicycle and was holding an expensive one alongside. Bolt cutters hung over his handle bars to form an upside down "V." In his drugged-out mind, the tool was a divining rod that discovered payday bikes rather than a water source.

He played his role exactly as expected.

"I didn't do nothin'. A guy sold it to me," he shouted at the surrounding cluster, while two of them took his picture.

There is a quote that, "A conservative is a liberal who's been mugged." By similar logic in this case, "A vigilante is an anarchist whose bike was stolen."

The incongruent philosophy of the two-wheeled cavalry was also expressed with how they unironically asserted individuality by sporting outfits that were the definition of sameness. Black cut-off jean shorts, a little too short for the men. Thriftshop boots or ratty shoes of another type. Armless jean jackets or vests, also black, adorned with various patches.

Each of them had the aroma of those who don't believe in laundry for clothing and soap for one's person. It was as if there was an unspoken competition to outreek each other. Curiously, the fake-bearded bike thief who lived in a squat house off St. Bernard smelled like roses by comparison.

Also of interest, despite their appearance and methods, the bike vigilantes were more effective than NOPD in deterring and solving bike theft. 911 calls backed up for multiple shifts made most crimes a low priority. This was the emerging legacy of Mayor Walter Vaccaro.

As Grange came upon the scene, which had the feel of impending violence, he saw the byproduct of exactly the reason he was in the Quarter. His eyes came to life.

He shoved the sign high to the sky and placed his bullhorn against quivering lips.

"End Whitesploitation!" he bleated, echoing the printed words. "All these movies are making us look bad. Like we're immature and stupid."

The swarm turned as one toward the intruder.

As they did, Grange noticed they all had one prominent patch in common, a round red one with a large centered "U," the letters "BG" in the middle, and lightning bolts on either side. Grange had no idea he was in the presence of the U-Lock Bike Gang, only that he had a new audience.

"I'm here to help you," he said. "You've all been poisoned by whitesploitation movies. TV shows too. They're making you act childish and silly. Less than human. Look at you all."

The bike gang vigilantes were indeed white, as was the bike thief they'd been accosting.

Those who claim the moral high horse rarely take to questioning of their motives. It was no different with the UBG. Especially when the one impugning them appeared as clean cut to have stepped out of the 1950's.

The clear leader spoke with indignation. "Who the fuck do you think you are? We're cleaning up the streets. Making this a better city."

Grange looked at them with pity and warbled into his bullhorn.

"I know you don't understand. I can tell. Your uniforms. Your bikes. Your silliness. Whitesploitation movies are making you act like children."

At this, all seven of them stepped off of their bikes. Those with thick chains draped around them jangled their concave or convex torsos. They proceeded toward Grange.

The bike thief could hardly believe his good luck. He quietly continued on in the opposite direction, riding one bike and ghostriding the second next to him.

Grange felt protected by his own moral high horse and more so his megaphone. "You're being exploited. All you white men."

An aggrieved voice rang out from the bike gang. "What about us women? Or however we identify?"

Grange had a ready answer.

"I've already identified you all. Poisoned by bad images. You don't know any better."

The vigilantes slowly moved closer. They might've been menacing except they most certainly weren't.

Grange wasn't sure if they were dangerous, though. "It's not your fault. We don't have the power. We're not the ones making the movies and TV shows. It's the New World Order," he sputtered.

A few cameras raised, chains rattled, and the ink of tattoos swirled in anticipation.

Morris Grange was prepared to start running, swinging his sign, or yelling for help, but none of those actions was necessary.

A long rough honk, equal parts Bronx cheer, Canadian goose, and Chalmette scream screeched down the block. Cabbie wanted to get through.

In an involuntary sigh of relief, Grange moved off to the side while murmuring under his breath, "Whew, that was close. I really need some meth now."

The gang had turned away from him to keep their bikes from getting run over, but a few of them spun back sharply. Grange had forgotten the bullhorn was amplifying everything he said.

The cabbie honked again. Longer this time.

Grange ambled along to the sidewalk, and the gang retrieved their chariots, ready for the next battle.

A few minutes later, the sign and bullhorn were in the backseat of Grange's car, and he was attempting to leave the French Quarter. That was not as simple as it sounds.

Even though several street signs throughout the city hadn't been replaced almost a decade after Hurricane Katrina, there was no lack of Road Closed signs.

The city was in the midst of a colliding series of infrastructure and redevelopment projects. Drainage all over Uptown. New streetcar line from Canal to Elysian Fields. Redoing the St. Charles streetcar line. Work by the Sewerage & Water Board and Entergy, the power company.

The city of New Orleans had become one big Detour Zone.

Although Grange exited the parking garage a block and a half from Canal, it took him over twenty minutes to follow the maze of traffic winding nine blocks out of his way to finally arrive at the wide main street.

He took a left at Claiborne shortly after.

His mind was partly on the last encounter. "I keep trying to help the people, but they don't want to hear," he said.

A few blocks later, Grange made a right turn on Tulane to head directly for a familiar spot.

"T-Eddie's always there. I really need to get high. It's been a stressful night. Gotta have that 8-ball," he bleated.

At 9:49 Grange entered a familiar parking lot. He paid $65 at the barred window off to the right side of the office and drove over to his room located on the lower level left-hand side.

Since the motel wasn't well lit at night, for good reason, he wasn't exactly sure which room was his, so he parked a few spots from the end.

Just before Grange readied himself to get out of the car, his excited hands dropped the electronic room key. "Damn," he said while rummaging at his feet to retrieve it.

While he was bent down, he heard a vehicle pull into the spot next to him, the engine cut off, and multiple doors open and close. Grange thought nothing of it. He was more concerned about his room key.

"Mwuh thuh fwuh kuh" was followed by someone being struck and an "Uhh!"

The sounds got Grange's attention. He kept his head down but looked up to the right.

His eyes lit like fireworks. A handful of men were leading a hooded person alongside Grange's car.

"I know what this is," he said to himself.

When they passed, he peeked over the windshield. The little procession was entering the room on the end.

Grange reflexively looked over at the vehicle they'd exited from and saw it was a white van. He put his car key in the ignition, but before he could start it, two men stepped out of the doorway on the end.

"Oh, shit," Grange said, ducking back down, trying to make himself as small and still as possible.

He soon heard them get into the van from the driver's and front passenger's doors, but the van stayed in place. Grange heard the low murmur of voices and smelled cigarette smoke.

He stayed hunched over and silent for what seemed an interminable time but was barely five minutes.

"It's happening," he kept repeating to himself.

Eventually the back doors of the van opened and closed before the vehicle pulled away. Grange was caught up in his fear, so he waited almost ten minutes to raise himself back up and look outside.

Complete silence.

It was an odd silence because the Capri Motel parking lot was usually witness to any sort of deal-arranging or outright arguing.

Grange slowly got out of his car, closed the door as quietly as he could, and crept toward the room on the end. As he got closer, he could see the door, just under the second floor staircase, was ajar.

"Oh, boy. Oh, boy," he whispered. "I could use that 8-ball."

When he got to the doorway, he saw a shabby door. It was blue, with a smattering of white paint on it. The number 138 was stenciled in white. A room key slot was midway up on the left, and a metal kick plate covered the bottom foot.

He leaned his upper body into the doorway and heard a groan from the floor.

Grange was frozen in place. No lights were on in the room, but he could make out that the prone figure was touching his hands to his wrists.

Grange next saw the man sit up and heard him clear his throat, spit, and say with disgust, "Gotdamn if they're not right for that."

In a soft scared voice, Grange called out from the doorway.

"I know what this is."

The man on the floor worked himself to his feet. "Who the hell are you? Part of this?" The anger in his voice was simmering.

"No, no," Grange said. "I was in the parking lot when they brought you in." "They didn't see me," he added.

The man walked up to Grange. His voice quickly reached boil.

"You part of this? I will fuck you up right now. Hear me?"

Grange shook his simple head from left to right, eyes wide, and mouth open.

"No, not me, but I know what happened."

The man studied Grange, coughed, and picked his nose. "Yeah," he said, all the heat out of his voice. "You couldn't do nothin' to nobody. Don't try me, though."

"I saw the white van they took you out of. I read about this. You were kidnapped by the New World Order," Grange offered.

"New World Order?" the man said. "Nah, this just some thugs, but you gonna help me find 'em. They don't even wanna know how I'm gonna turn up. And I will, good as my name's Leon Sparks."

Grange thought to himself about how most people treated him with contempt, about how he knew it really was the N.W.O. despite what the guy said, and about how he could be of use. He wasn't so keen about helping out the man in front of him rubbing his wrists, though, but he wasn't going to say that.

"Well, here, let me tell you what I saw, then I'll get out of your way," Grange said, edging from the doorway.

"No," Sparks said. "Right about now, I need some sleep. You gonna help me in the morning. We findin' 'em. Gimme your keys."

Without waiting for a response, Sparks pulled Grange inside, grabbed keys that he pushed into the toe of his left shoe, closed the door, and pointed to the bed for Grange before Sparks himself stretched out on the floor, blocking the door.

Chapter 4

Bobby Delery felt lightheaded while Tiny drove him home. It wasn't the cognac but the news about his family.

His New Orleans roadway pet peeves didn't have the usual effect on Delery. He wasn't bothered by the driver in front of them who poked along at half the speed limit before running a red, leaving them stuck at the light they easily could have made.

He wasn't even bothered when they crossed Franklin and saw a train ahead blocking St. Claude, but Tiny was.

"These trains. We're not waiting," he said as he made a U-turn through a neutral ground intersection to go back to Franklin and take it up and across the Robertson overpass above the tracks.

Norfolk Southern operated what was commonly known as The Bywater Train. It was legally restricted to only block the tracks ten minutes if moving and five if still.

Twenty to thirty minute waits were more the usual. In some cases, the thorn in the side of the neighborhood was twisted further by a cumulative blocking for most of an hour.

As they went across the overpass, Delery rose slightly out of his haze, recalling the first time he'd seen Miss Melba Barnes, resplendent all in white on her way to church. She was carrying a big beer case full of close to a million dollars that'd shown up in her yard by happenstance. Though he'd been called by NOPD to assist them in recovery of the money his first day back in town, he'd ultimately done what he thought was best and helped Miss Melba distribute the cash to worthy organizations after it had been laundered at the casino.

He'd told no one. Hadn't talked to Ellis about it. "Maybe some day," he thought. "Maybe one day I will."

A few minutes later, Tiny dropped him off at his Dauphine Street apartment between Montegut and Clouet. Only two blocks and a levee from the river.

Tiny promised to call and check on him. The fresh spring breeze Delery felt while walking from the car to the front door did nothing to improve his disposition.

"Oh, baby. Are you okay?" Ellis called out as she quickly marched to the front when he entered.

"I've been better," Delery said weakly.

Ellis' left hand cradled his head and her right held his left arm. She looked directly at his face and for a moment thought it resembled a house with his long sad eyes as two dormer windows.

"You're really in your feelings. What happened, Bobby?"

They walked over to the grey sofa with vertical white pinstripes that was further inside the parlor of his one bedroom shotgun and sat down.

Delery alternated between looking at Ellis, off in space, and at his own hands while he relayed back what he'd learned from Tiny. The only part he left out was some of the goriness surrounding the killings of Isaac, his family, and Curtis.

"I didn't know," he said in a cracking voice. "They were here in New Orleans. Why would my dad lie to me?"

"Is there anyone else in your family to talk to? So you can know and have closure?" she asked.

"Don't think so. One of the first things I learned in criminology is that everybody wants closure. Solving a case is working toward closure. A lot of times, though, you don't get it. That's just how it is. Closure's a modern concept. Life's more ambiguous, like it or not."

Delery paused, not sure whether he should keep going. He decided to.

"I don't expect to ever know why my dad did that, but I will be getting in touch with a man who might be able to help me find out why my brothers got killed."

Ellis hardened her face.

"No, Bobby. There are dangerous people here. You can't do this," she said. "You know how black men spend so much time and effort trying to keep yourselves from violence. Don't walk right into it."

"What, you think I'm gonna go shoot somebody and keep perpetuating the cycle? C'mon. I will get justice, though. New Orleans is too small. Somebody knows something."

She scoffed. "If you find out who did it, you're gonna rely on the legal system? Assuming you can get admissible evidence."

"Like I said," he emphasized. "I'm not gonna kill anybody, but I have to do this. Do you know what it feels like to come back to New Orleans, keep my career going and meet you, only to find out that at some point the truth about my family was bound to come out. I'd have found out eventually. If not Tiny, somebody else. Who knows what other grim shit happened I don't know about yet."

"You can't think that way," she said. "It'll eat you up inside."

"I'm already eaten up," he said. "The man who raised me was nothing but a liar. Everyone else is dead. All I have is you. Right?"

"Of course," she said. "I love you, Bobby."

"Ellis, I love you too," he said.

Delery added, "I won't do anything crazy. I'll be careful. You have to understand, though. I can't let this be. For my own sake. My own sanity."

Ellis reached out and took both his hands with her own.

"I know," she said. "But I don't want to lose you. Don't make me regret what I said."

"The word?" he asked.

"Mmm hmm. The big word," she agreed.

"I liked hearing that." Delery leaned his head back. "I'll get through this. Right now I could use some food."

They left the house. While Delery locked up, Ellis said, "I sat outside and read a bit. Feels so good out here. Your neighbors are friendly."

His mind on other things, Delery replied automatically, "Yeah? Which ones?"

She pointed to the blue double shotgun house on the immediate right. "The couple there."

He became more alert. "Wait. The two here on the end? She has a bob. He wears thick retro glasses."

She nodded. "They got home. Said hello. We made a little small talk."

His volume increased. "You've got to be kidding me. They've lived here at least two months and haven't said a word to me. Walk right on by. I've said hello to them twice and they totally blew me off."

Ellis reached her right hand out. "Bobby, it's alright. No big deal."

Delery continued thundering. "I've seen 'em say hello to Mr. Verdine down the block. Chocolate-colored old man. But the rest of the block's white and they don't say a thing to anyone else."

"Bobby you're getting worked up. They're gonna hear you. Some people aren't very friendly. That's how it is."

He shook his head vehemently.

"It's partly about that. People moving here for the New Orleans thing but not realizing that being friendly to your neighbors and greeting strangers *is* the New Orleans thing."

He lowered his voice in response to her right hand signaling him to take his level down.

"Not just that, Ellis. The white couple would rather be thought unfriendly assholes than racists. You think it's random they don't say hello to anyone else but you and Mr. Verdine? They don't know I'm black, so they've been blowing me off. They think I'm white. Rather be thought unfriendly to white people than racist to black people. Damn."

Ellis tilted her head and turned her mouth as well. "Progress?"

Delery shrugged. "Maybe so, but it's messed up. Let's walk."

They turned to the left and walked a little less than two blocks downriver to the corner of Dauphine and Louisa. Passed the large historic Father Seelos church along the way, known for its Spanish Mass. Passed a variety of colorfully painted houses.

Delery looked up at the sign hanging alongside the restaurant at the corner.

"Friday," he read.

"I heard about this," Ellis said. "The name changes to match the day of the week. Looks like they change the sign every day too."

Delery's eyes narrowed.

"I know," she said. "Not just that. The menus are on calendars. There's a different menu for each day. The food and drinks are all named after famous people born that day of the week."

"Good Lord, that won't last," he scoffed.

"Look," she said, gesturing with her head toward the windows.

Friday was packed. The crowd inside seemed absolutely up to their elbows in bliss.

"I can't tell who lives here and who's a tourist," he said.

"You don't even want to know," she said, continuing a couple steps to turn left on Louisa. "In the article, the owners were talking like they're the saviors of the neighborhood, the hub of the Bywater renaissance."

"Seriously?" he asked. "This is nothing but a corny gimmick.

I don't expect every restaurant to be a po boy joint, but come on."

"Remember though, the trendier it is, the quicker it burns out. We're going to Captain Sal's, right?" she asked.

Delery nodded. "Good Friday crawfish," he said.

Louisa Street between Dauphine and Burgundy was their favorite block in the neighborhood. Plenty of trees for shade. A range of architectural styles. Interesting landscaping in a couple cases.

When they reached the end of the block, they continued on two more to the restaurant. There were numerous establishments of this type throughout the city, but Captain Sal's was the closest and the food was good.

At the corner to their right was a daiquiri bar, directly across the street a dollar store, and a tire shop on the kitty corner. Delery and Ellis made a left and walked to the front door that faced St. Claude. He pulled firmly to open the door, knowing it had a habit of sticking.

A couple tables off to the right were occupied with eaters, but most of the five people sitting or standing in that area were waiting on orders to come up. Three others stood in a loose line in front of the two cash registers.

Though many ordered menu choices as if Sal's was no more than a fast food joint, Delery only ate whatever was boiled in mouth-tingling spices. He looked over at the warming pans. Shrimp, pig feet, turkey necks, bags of corn and also potatoes.

Five large clear rectangular containers sat on the far end of the counter. They were filled with boiled crawfish.

Delery watched the young Asian man walk from the cash register with a clear plastic bag, open the container, fill a large scoop, and deposit its contents into the bag. He carried the bag over to place it onto a scale alongside the register. 2.59 pounds. Close enough to the order of two and a half pounds.

Before he could tie up the bag and return the scoop to the top container, the man who'd placed the order before Delery and Ellis entered called out, "Give me another pound."

This was a typical request, and the restaurant employee dutifully added more crawfish to the bag.

Delery too thought nothing of it and only casually observed that the customer was wearing a yellow reflective safety vest with orange stripes over a white t-shirt. Instinctively he and everyone else inside Sal's knew the young man had just gotten off work.

Delery also noticed the man had a black spandex do-rag on his head and crisp blue suede high top sneakers on his feet. Delery was indifferent enough to not hazard a guess that the customer must've changed from dirty boots into the expensive blue shoes after work.

"Bobby, what all are you getting?" Ellis asked.

"We won't eat enough to get a break on the price for ten pounds," Delery said. "I'm thinking five pounds, bag of corn, bag potatoes."

His lack of interest in anything but his family and appetite changed when the guy in the vest turned and walked past them to leave. The man was looking down at his food and didn't see Delery register surprise.

"Chin beard and neck tattoo of a lion. I know him," Delery quickly thought.

His mind raced back to about ten months before, both when he was canvassing the streets near St. Ferdinand for a chalky white man and then outside Harrah's Casino witnessing a shootout.

Delery stabbed his hand into a random pocket and came up with a twenty dollar bill that he thrust into Ellis' hand.

"Go ahead and place my order. Wait inside. I think I recognize…"

He turned abruptly to follow the man who was halfway out the door, but he was not so hasty to keep Ellis from observing an intense look in his eyes she'd not seen before.

"Excuse me. Excuse me," Delery practically spat out as he vaulted down the three steps toward the guy heading directly to a car parked in front of Sal's.

The man in the safety vest glanced back casually toward Delery with no recognition. He continued to his car but waited for passing traffic to get around on the driver's side.

"We need to talk," said Delery once he ended up next to him.

"No. Go way."

Instead of discouraging Delery, hearing the man speak made him more confident he was right. He stepped over in front of him, almost into the street. The stress of his family news had him wound up.

"I'm not going any fucking where," Delery said, talking hard.

The man was thinking, "What I gotta do to this punk? Better check himself," when Delery spoke again, this time in a stage whisper.

"I know you. You and your friend tried to rob me on the street last year. Also saw you kill two guys in front of Harrah's. If you leave, I'll get your license plate number. Now you gonna talk?"

"You a cop?"

Delery shook his head, not mentioning he was a criminologist who worked with NOPD.

The man, who didn't look to be out of his twenties, first peered around before telling Delery, "Don't ruin this for me, man. That thing on Canal Street fucked me up. Them dudes I shot disappeared. Saw on TV the only body left was that dead bouncer and they put that on my boy Stink cuz he got hit. Couldn't move. That's some bullshit."

"You left him there to take the rap," accused Delery.

The man known on the street as Blue Shoes raised his voice. "He ain't shot the bouncer!"

He looked around and lowered his voice.

"Stink ain't shot him. No jacket neither. Why they gonna put it on him? We was walkin' along 'n saw 'em takin' the bouncer. Men standin' up for our kind. No way them ballistics matched. What I'm gonna do? Wait there? 'Hello Officer, cuff me.' Stink got put in Angola on some bullshit."

"It's not right. Like I said, I saw it happen, but you know how the system works. They're gonna pin it on somebody," Delery said.

"Whoa," Blue Shoes said, raising his hand. "You knew Stink's innocent and you said nothin'?"

Delery thought quickly, not wanting to reveal that he hadn't wanted extra attention on what he was doing at the casino. He decided to deflect.

"You didn't say anything either. Didn't read in the news about you testifying in court on his behalf."

Blue Shoes narrowed his eyes.

"We both done wrong 'cept it fucked up my head and you don't give a shit. But I'm tryin'. Tryin'-a do better."

He tapped his vest.

"Got me a regular job. Them docks up by Tchoupitoulas. Don't need no more bullshit."

"Good for you, " Delery said. "I mean that."

"Yeah, I got two weeks left-a put in my ninety days. Then I'm-a official longshoreman," he said.

"What exactly do you do?" asked Delery.

Blue Shoes huffed. "Whatta you think? This country. Bet you don't know where our steel comes from?"

Remembering all the Midwestern job layoffs when he was a kid, Delery shook his head.

"Korea. Least what I work on. 'Less it's raining. Only thing worse 'n that's the refrigerated boat. You know we send chicken to Russia?"

"Really? There aren't chicken farms in Europe?" wondered Delery.

"Dunno. But that's what I do. Tryin'-a do better. You not gonna go to the po-lice, huh?"

Delery looked at Blue Shoes, seeing the seriousness and vulnerability in his eyes.

"No. How could I? You're working to build something with your life. How can I not respect that?"

Blue Shoes felt immense relief but was confused.

"Why you wanna convo? I mean, if you not after something," he said.

Delery left out that he was still confused about how the entire story fit together. Thinking of the concept of closure he'd talked about earlier with Ellis, he'd probably never know. That reminded him of the present.

"There is another thing. You were out there hustlin'. Know of a Curtis Delery?"

"What's he to you?" Blue Shoes asked suspiciously.

"He's my brother," Delery said softly. "Somebody killed him about a year ago."

"Wow. You want it 100, least what I know? Your brother he liked the H. Feel me? I heard—this a rumor—but I heard he was a snitch for the po-lice. Sorry, but real talk," said Blue Shoes.

"A lot of people might've been gunning for him," added Delery to complete the thought.

"Yeah," said Blue Shoes.

Delery didn't make aloud the next thing that came to mind. "If Curtis was killed for being a C.I., then why go after Isaac and his family too?" he wondered.

"I'm not gonna keep you any longer. Good luck," he said and shook hands with Blue Shoes.

"'Precciate that. Bust my ass at work but my kicks always gonna be on point. Nobody on pluck like me. I'm ghost."

Blue Shoes went on his way and Delery turned toward Captain Sal's to see Ellis watching him with concern from inside the front door.

Chapter 5

Morris Grange was in the midst of a nightmare. He was running along cliffs overlooking an ocean, but his right foot kept getting caught by hands that reached up from the rock.

He awoke with a start and jumped again when he saw a standing Leon Sparks tapping and pulling at his foot. It was Saturday.

"Get up, man," Sparks said. "Don't make me touch this no more. What the hell you got on your feet? These sneaks from the discount store?"

Suddenly it all came back to Grange. The meth mission that never came about, the abduction ending he witnessed, and being stuck in the room with a stranger.

"What kind of shoes are *you* wearing?" he blurted out defensively.

Sparks smirked and lifted his right foot up on the end of the bed.

"Two-tone alligator skin. Italian made. *These* are pretty."

Grange sat up, rubbed his eyes, ran his hands through his hair, and looked at the man with bent leg in front of him.

"I don't care about any of that," Grange warbled. "I just want to go home."

Sparks removed his foot and folded his arms.

"Triflin'," he said, shaking his head. "You were here last night to get your freak on or get high. Maybe both. Before you go home, you gonna help me find the motherfuckers tried to do me harm. Threatened me."

Grange tried to reply, "But you…"

"No, you gonna help me. Think I wanna spend my Saturday with your triflin' ass. Listen, you don't know me. I don't wanna know you. But I'll tell ya, Morris Grange…"

Grange quickly checked his right back pocket for his leather wallet. Sparks pointed to the nightstand.

"Needed to find out who you were," Sparks said. "Your little play money's all there."

Grange reached over, grabbed his wallet, and opened it.

Sparks continued. "Like I was saying, you don't know me, but black don't crack. Ebony, onyx, jet. None of 'em. Me myself, I'm gonna find out where they took me in that white van. You gonna help. Right now I need you to do one thing, Morris. Can you do that for me?"

The use of first name and the question of assistance was a car salesman tactic at developing familiarity and connection. Sparks had a different context in mind, though.

Grange was suspicious. To him it was some sort of gay proposition. His mind raced. He put his palms out and extended his arms.

"I'm not into that," he bleated resolutely.

Sparks laughed deeply from his belly. The cheap room shook as if from a tremor.

"He's not into that." Sparks could barely get it out.

He gestured to himself. "You lookin' at a man who's into pussy, alright? A player to the bone. That's how they tricked me. Only thing I need you to do is man the fuck up. Then you go home in time to hunt for Easter eggs tomorrow."

"Okay," Grange said softly.

"Say it," Sparks pushed.

"Say what?" Grange asked.

"Say you're gonna man the fuck up. Come on. We gotta go."

Grange felt alarm again. "Wait a minute. Go where?"

"Go find where they took me. Where else? You think I'm gonna call my employees? Tell 'em some foul shit happened to their boss? They'd lose respect. No, they not gonna be involved."

He gestured with his head at Grange. "You are, Morris. And what you gonna do?"

"Man up," Grange said in the same small warbly voice.

"Gonna what?" Sparks demanded louder.

"I'm gonna man up," Grange said with more volume.

"Say it like you mean it," Sparks threatened.

Grange cleared his throat. With firm bleat, he said, "I'll man up right now."

Sparks nodded. "My man. Go wash your face and do your business so we can get goin'."

When Grange stepped out of the bathroom, Sparks jingled keys at him.

"You're drivin'. Takin' your car. I need to concentrate."

Sparks looked at the keys. "This one here looks like the house key, so I'm puttin' it in my pocket for now. 'Til this thing is done."

Grange was about to speak, but Sparks cut him off.

"Look, I know you don't like me. I definitely don't like you. But it is what it is. We got common purpose, Morris."

Grange walked to the door.

"Common purpose. Vengeance."

Sparks walked behind Grange to the car, unlocked the driver's side door to let Grange in, and kept the keys while he went around to the passenger side and let himself in.

While Sparks was getting in and looking at the contents of the back seat, Grange saw the room key at his feet and remembered more of the previous night.

"I need to check out of my room," he said, while simultaneously Sparks called out, "Gotdamn if I ain't seen everything."

He pulled Grange's "End Whitesploitation!" sign to the front. "The hell is this?" Sparks asked.

Grange chose his words carefully.

"The state tax credits for movies take too much of our money," he said.

Sparks tapped the sign. "Don't lie on me. That's not what the sign says."

Grange continued. "Have you been to the movies lately? All they do anymore is make white people look silly, less than human. They're exploiting us."

Sparks repeated, "Less than human." He sighed. "Mmm hmm. Let me get this right. White folks get exploited by Hollywood?"

"TV too," Grange added.

"So, Morris. Who exactly is doin' the exploitin'? Who runs Hollywood?"

Grange spoke freely. "My people, white people, don't have the power."

"Oh, Lord. Morris, who has the power? All the black brothers runnin' Hollywood?"

Grange looked startled. "Of course. And liberals too. It's turned into..."

Sparks stopped him. "I barely been knowin' you, but damn if it just keeps gettin' better. You freaky junkie, you." He tossed the sign to the back seat.

Grange was frozen to say any more.

"Don't drive too fast once you get goin', Morris. Maintain 25-30 mph. That was the speed they drove," said Sparks.

He closed his eyes and slightly tilted his head forward.

"What are you doing?" Grange asked.

"Closin' my eyes to repeat the experience when they had me in that van. See if the streets can talk. Usin' my senses," Sparks replied. "I was keepin' track of turns and how long we went. Problem is you can make it anywhere in New Orleans in about twenty minutes, least 'fore all-a this construction."

"Why don't you use your phone to track the map?" Grange

asked. "It'll work better."

Sparks opened his eyes and stared at the younger man.

"Don't make me tear you up 'fore we get started," Sparks said menacingly. "And I heard what you said 'bout your room. No checkin' out yet. Get the car started. 25-30 mph. Mind my directions."

Grange started the car and backed out.

"When I was a kid, used to close my eyes on the bus, see if I could figure out which street we turned on, light we stopped at, what have you. Neighbor kid was blind, and I wanted to know what it was like. Could I still see colors like my crayon colors?" Sparks said.

He closed his eyes again.

"They put a hood on me, but we gonna figure out where they went. First turn is a right out the parking lot."

Before Grange could make the turn, Sparks added, "They made a left after a block or so. Get over in the left lane."

"This is a wild goose chase. There's construction all across the street. How can I make a left turn?" Grange complained.

"I saw it on the way here. Tore all those houses down for medical facilities when Big Charity Hospital sits vacant. All to get federal dollars and save walkin' a few blocks. Plus, don't think they're not tryin' to change Tulane and the rest-a these streets. You just get ready for a left turn."

They passed a few more no-tell motels on the right mixed with some shiny new condos, while the footprint of the medical complex under construction sprawled across the left.

"No left yet?" asked Sparks.

"Not yet," bleated Grange. "But up ahead looks like one. There's a sign, though. No left turn."

"Don't matter," said Sparks casually. "That's gotta be our turn. I remember after that it's a straight shot for awhile."

"Wait a minute. I'm not making an illegal turn. What if

NOPD pulls us over and sees my…"

Grange stopped speaking, remembering he hadn't actually bought the 8-ball. He was giving too much information away.

"First, you make that turn, or I put a foot to your ass. Hear me? I'll make it myself if I gotta. Second, if the po-lice are anywhere on this street, they're waiting outside the Mexican clubs to get cash off all them day laborers," said Sparks.

Grange sighed, muttered that those clubs were mostly filled with Hondurans, flipped his signal, and made a left onto the intersecting one-way street.

"Good, good. What's this?" Sparks asked.

"Galvez. I turned like you said," Grange answered, happy to change the conversation.

"I remember a straight shot for a bit," said Sparks while he opened his eyes and checked his watch. "10:47 right now. Road was mostly smooth. A few streetlights along the way. We gonna hit a bump up there 'fore too long."

Grange nodded, grimacing.

Sparks rubbed his hands together. "Morris Gump talkin' slick. You're not holdin', are you?"

"My last name's Grange. You think I never heard Gump before? Real original, Leon." Grange added too emphatically, "And no, I'm not holding. I forgot, okay."

Sparks looked at him knowingly. "That's why you went to Capri. Lookin' to score. What you use, Morris?"

"I don't see why this is any of your damn business," Grange shot off.

"Morris, you may as well talk. We got all day."

Grange tossed his left hand into the air.

"Okay, damn. Meth. I smoke meth. You happy?"

Sparks grinned from ear to ear. "Oh, mercy. Jesus take the wheel. Meth-head with a whitesploitation sign. Damn, Morris Gump. Can you be any more obvious?"

Sparks laughed. Grange was silent.

"So, Captain Obvious, you gonna take that 8-ball over by the trailer park and smoke it with your kin while watchin' NASCAR, least 'til you get a little thirsty for your cousin?" Sparks said.

In his frustration and anger, Grange had a rare breakthrough of logic.

"Wait a minute. Why'd you get kidnapped, Leon. If it wasn't the New World Order, then why would anyone want you?"

It was Sparks' turn for silence.

Grange kept going. "You're either a pimp or a drug dealer. I'm guessing drug dealer."

"Enough-a that shit," Sparks answered. "I'm a businessman. Run a car lot. On the up and up."

Grange smiled, firm in his conclusion. "Oh no, Leon. You're a drug dealer who got kidnapped. They didn't kill you, so they either robbed you or want a cut."

Sparks raised his voice. "Black man equals drug dealer, huh?"

"In this case it sure does, Captain Obvious," said Grange smugly.

"That's some bullshit, Morris. Keep on, smart mouth."

Grange's mind was unexpectedly twitching and activating, so another notion came to him.

"Wait, Leon. You don't have any meth on you, huh?"

Sparks shot back, "Hell no. That's redneck shit. Not my clientele." He paused and said softer, "You think you're slick. Just drive."

"That's what I thought," answered Grange. "Wish you had an 8-ball, though."

When the Esplanade light turned green, Grange continued on. A couple minutes later they came to another light at the St. Bernard intersection.

Sparks peeked at his watch. "10:52," he said. "Goin' off to

the right after this intersection. See how it curves around. They must've went this way."

He closed his eyes again and concentrated.

"There's nothin' I heard or smelled along the way. The road, though. It tells the tale. In another minute or so it's gonna get real bad. They had to slow the van down, so we'll know. Keep stayin' on Galvez."

Grange quietly followed directions and bleated in affirmation when they hit a stretch that was filled with so many dips and hops as to seem intentional.

"See, this is it," Sparks said, pleased to be on the right path.

Grange sniffed. "New Orleans has terrible roads. It's not like this in Metairie."

"It's not like New Orleans at all," Sparks both agreed and jabbed. "This city definitely don't care 'bout the roads. Good for the auto business, though," he mused.

Once they returned to an even surface, Sparks asked. "What's our next main street?"

"We're about to pass Franklin, " Grange answered.

"Morris, should be a bridge real soon. Not a big one. See a bridge yet?"

"No, there's no...wait. There's an overpass coming up," said Grange.

"Good, good," said Sparks. "You go over that bridge. I'm-a keep my eyes closed. A few blocks past the bridge, make a left. We gotta be 'bout there."

Grange drove along the overpass that spanned the train yard. He looked along the left side as the car descended.

"Not the first blocks?" he asked.

"Dunno, but I don't think so," said Sparks. "Wait a few blocks, then turn. Look for a vacant building. Big enough to fit big cages inside"

When they were back on the ground, Grange said, "We

can't turn on Clouet. No left turn. I'm not turning into traffic on a one-way street, Leon."

"I don't think we're there yet, but you gonna turn whatever direction I need you to. Hear me?"

Another block passed. "Another one-way. Can't make a left on Louisa either."

"No problem," said Sparks. They didn't make that left 'til a few blocks. We'll try the first one we come to. We're close. I can feel it."

At the next intersection, Grange called out, "We can turn left here. This is Piety Street." He read aloud the restaurant sign at the corner, "Poppa's Seafood."

"Alright," Sparks nodded. "I remember the road was smooth for a couple-a blocks after the turn. Got bumpy then."

Grange realized he hadn't been nervous at all before, thinking the expedition no more than a fruitless drive.

"What if we find the kidnappers?" he thought.

"Leon, this can't be it," he said. "This is residential. Little houses and empty lots. I don't see anything big and blighted. Only some boarded up houses."

"Shh!" Sparks insisted. He put both palms out to balance his senses and memory. "It's the reverse. This stretch of road was bumpy first and smooth after that. I don't think this is it, but keep goin'"

Grange continued driving and felt his anxiety rise.

"Okay, stop!" Sparks shouted. He opened his eyes, checked his watch, and looked around. "11:02. It's the right amount-a time, but this ain't the street. No building on the corner. We made one last left. They stopped after that."

A vacant lot with recently cut grass covered the entire block on the left. Overgrown lots on the right alternated with boarded up houses, most barely standing. Across the intersection, a row of single shotgun houses dotted the left while weeds and trees stretched up over twenty feet tall on the right.

"Nah, wrong street," said Sparks. "Take this one-way to the left and loop back 'round."

When Grange turned left on Galvez to try again, he cut off a car proceeding at a fast clip. The driver pushed the brake to slow down.

"Look at that, Erykah," she said. "People drive foolish like this in Baton Rouge?"

"They sure do," the daughter replied to her mother Maggie Asbury.

The two of them were on their way to Saturday brunch. In the next block Erykah saw a man hunched and walking while only wearing his drawers. "Oh, Lord," she said, guessing correctly that he'd just been robbed at gunpoint and forced to strip.

Chapter 6

For a long moment their eyes locked and held, each one searching the other.

They both moved forward in unison as if choreographed. Ellis pushing the Captain Sal's door open to leave with a big bag of food. Delery walking away from the curb while Blue Shoes drove off on St. Claude.

"You're worrying me!" she called out, bridging the seven steps between them.

He tried to calm her. "Don't worry."

The edge remained in her voice. "I saw you go at that guy. Who was he?"

"Don't worry," he repeated. "Just somebody I remembered who might have some information about my brother."

They turned toward Louisa to head back to Delery's place. "Did he?"

"No, probably not."

"Bobby, you can't start questioning every person who looks like he's been in the streets," Ellis urged.

"I know. I won't. But this guy…I remembered him. Looks like he's getting his life on track."

"Okay," she said, still looking at him with concern.

A few minutes later they were out back at Delery's. Both of them hovered over the boiled food spilled out across a newspaper covered table. A roll of paper towels stood off to the side. Two beer bottles rose from amidst the crawfish.

They expertly twisted off the tails, sucked the occasional fat from the heads, and broke the segments along the tails to eat the meat before discarding the shells and moving on to the next.

Neither wore surgical gloves, gardening gloves, or any of that nonsense. What you did was you wiped your hands off with paper towels and washed when you were done. You knew some cayenne pepper would remain for a few hours, so that wasn't the best time to do something like take out your contacts.

All that came with the territory. If you looked like a clown, your crawfish game was weak. You were living in the wrong city.

When they finished, the contents of the table were all wrapped up in the newspapers and pushed off into a trash bag that went directly into the oversized wheeled receptacle up front.

"Ellis, I need some time to sit and think. It was a crazy day," Delery said.

She was unmoved from her previous concern.

"You're sure? Nothing rash?" she asked.

"No, it's fine. I'm mentally and emotionally exhausted. Probably go to bed early."

They held each other and kissed, each feeling the added spiciness of the other's crawfish lips and tongues.

"Love you, bae. I really do," he said.

"Love you too," she said. "Talk to you tomorrow, okay?"

He nodded. "Need to get my head clear."

Delery watched her leave. She was a couple inches shorter than his 5'10", enough to make her the same height or taller if she had on heels. Was wearing her hair above her ears and more natural these days.

Though he felt hollow from the shocking news about his family, he knew he had a golden lady in his life.

"I've dated a lot of women over the years, but we fit," he thought before going right back to his hurt and confusion.

Though Delery was worried about tainting good music with bad feelings, he needed vinyl accompaniment. After thumbing through his records, he pulled out Stevie Wonder's *Innervisions* and *Places* by Jan Garbarek. Added the Phil Cohran joint he'd purchased earlier.

These and beer to sip made the rest of his evening.

He slept fitfully, unable to settle into deep restful sleep. When he woke up on Saturday, he felt like he'd just gone to bed.

All the questions and anxiety that had plagued him the previous day were foremost in his mind the second his eyes opened.

Why had his dad lied to him? Was Tiny lying to him? Covering for Isaac? No, that could easily be proven. Why had his brothers been killed? Why had his parents divorced? Had that affected Curtis and made him more susceptible to getting hooked on heroin? Would he ever know any of these answers? Should he have stayed in Chicago? Ignorance is bliss. Or is it?

"All that to drink didn't help," Delery muttered while walking back to retrieve some aspirin for his headache.

After a long morning routine, he made his way up front to find what he'd not done before stumbling into bed. The Stevie record was left on the turntable.

He'd known that since moving back he was becoming a little less fussy about certain things, taking on more of a necessary laidback attitude. Bending to New Orleans was often the best way to stay sane. He remembered reading a quote in a news story from a woman whose stretch of New Orleans East hadn't seen needed city investment post-Katrina and was still a mess. "Laissez faire's gonna bless us or kill us. Maybe both," she'd said.

Delery gently lifted the record up by the middle so as not to touch the playing surface and slid it into the protective sleeve inside the right side of the gatefold. He looked at the artwork on the back cover. Scanned the song titles and was embarrassed to tear up when he read "Living For The City" and thought of the lyrics.

"Nothing else makes sense, but these are gonna be alphabetized," he said, placing *Innervisions* into its protective plastic sleeve and taking it with the other two records over to their proper places.

Delery didn't bother to shave, but cleaned up. The clock showed 10:55 a.m. He checked the address Tiny gave him for Z, who supposedly would be able to help. Now was as good a time as any to catch a person who didn't keep regular office hours.

It only took him a few minutes to drive upriver a little stretch and follow the St. Claude curve. He saw the address on the right, but since there was no parking there he continued to St. Bernard, made a right, and parked in the first available spot, an angled one next to King Supermarket.

Traffic on St. Bernard had the usual flow for that time of day. He was more interested in a shabbily dressed man in a blue drum major hat pedaling toward Claiborne in the bike lane on what looked like it would cost Delery two months rent.

Delery walked back around. His destination was between a new corner market and an old tire shop. It was an ugly cinderblock building with white siding across the front and a door on the right side. He peeked around to the side of the building. No windows. Entirely painted white. A few red graffiti tags.

He stepped back to the front. Plywood fit in place halfway up the door to cover broken glass. Above it read the street number and "Orbis Security."

Looked like no one had been there for some time, but Delery pulled the handle to try just in case. He'd driven there, so why not?

He was surprised when it gave way to the hermetic cube.

Delery stepped inside and closed the door. He surveyed the room with a glance.

Spartan space. White walls. Laminate floor tile. Mold spots on the drop-ceiling. Framed picture of Malcolm X. Grey file cabinet next to a wooden desk. Man seated behind the desk looking up in thought. Head turned sideways making the tilt of his blue Kangol even more pronounced. Pen in his right hand. Two chairs on the door side of the desk. No other doors, so no restroom, storage, or other rooms.

Delery gestured with an index finger toward an empty chair, a wordless query to sit down.

The man, presumably Z.A. Marais, remained in concentration and shook his own index fingers. Not at Delery but as if working out a problem in his mind.

Delery took the liberty of walking five steps over to a chair and sat in it. His movement triggered the other man's attention.

"Excuse my manners," Delery said.

"No, you're good," was the reply while the man put his pen down. "I'm over here cursing everything but God. Trying to think of a word. You need directions?"

It was Delery's turn to look quizzical. "Directions? No, I'm here for your help. Aren't you Z.A. Marais? Brotherman?"

The other man studied Delery through eyes that peeked from under lids that looked like blinds pulled down to keep out the sunlight. The intense gaze and goatee seemed to double the photo of the former Malcolm Little if the revolutionary leader had been of darker complexion and worn contacts instead of his iconic browline glasses. This was not lost on Bobby Delery.

"Yes, I'm Marais. Sorry to say I'm all booked up, though."

"Tiny referred me. Said you were the one to talk to for help," Delery tried again.

"How do you know Tiny?" Marais asked, testing him.

"He was the best friend of my brother Isaac. Ever since they were babies."

"Whoa. Your *brother*? Isaac Delery's brother died. Same day he did."

Delery gave a brief explanation of what had brought him to the little office. He explained why he was so light-skinned and left out any mention of what his father had concealed.

"You're a Delery, huh?" Marais said, as much to himself as across the desk. "You got one drop, but that's all. You know what they say about the zebra, Bobby?"

Delery shook his head left to right.

"Doesn't matter if it's black with white stripes or white with black stripes. It's a zebra. Is what it is," Marais answered.

He stood up, winced a bit, and extended his hand to shake Delery's. As Delery stood-in-kind and met Marais' welcome, he noticed the man couldn't be an inch taller than 5'5".

They both sat down, and Marais rediscovered his pen and previous quandary. "I was trying to find the perfect word. See, I've read lots of books. Read enough to know plenty of relevant and irrelevant information. Read enough to know why things happen the way they do. Got me?"

Delery nodded.

"I don't need to read anymore, Bobby. What I do now is write about books I've always hoped to read. Ones I wish would be written. Sounds silly, I know, but hey, that's how I pass the time. 'All human evil comes from man's inability to sit quietly in a room.' That's a quote by Pascal. "

He lifted his left leg and rubbed his ankle.

"Sprained it on the way here," he said. "Okay, your brother. I mean, brothers. Not sure what I can do that NOPD hasn't. Cases are cold, right?"

Delery agreed. "Yes, but what I'm looking for is three pieces of information. The detectives working both Isaac and Curtis' murders. Second, Curtis' parole officer."

He paused.

Marais used the moment to ask, "But Bobby, you can find all that out yourself."

"Sure, it'll be the first thing I learn," Delery agreed. "But I want to know about them. Reps. Are they clean? Reasonably clean, anyway. I've been away long enough to not know about anybody."

"Got it," Marais said.

"There's more to this. Isaac, Curtis, and Isaac's wife and kids all killed the same day. Especially shady the way it was done."

Marais nodded again. "True."

Delery explained the third item he was looking for.

"That's gonna take a little longer," Marais said. "Should be able to find out without it costing much. You realize that's how it works. If I pay, you pay."

"Of course," Delery replied.

"Good. Let's work the money thing out. Don't worry. I'm here to help my people and make a little scratch. Keep the roof overhead. Won't nobody tell you I'm not fair."

The first hint of a smile crept into Marais' eyes, briefly breaking his serious demeanor.

"Now Bobby, let me get your number. Won't be too long for word on NOPD and the parole officer. Be strong. But realize…"

He spoke with measured words.

"Realize some real bad men did this to your family. You said you're a criminologist. Nobody talked, not even NOPD's paid snitches or for that Crimestoppers reward. There's a reason for that. Ain't no sloppy little clique here."

"I know," Delery said.

"Now let me tell you what I was working on here before you showed up. I'm writing about a book—imaginary, remember—about people who tell the truth. I know that doesn't sound like much, does it?"

Delery shook his head.

"There are liars all over the place, of course, but the ones who really interest me are the truth-tellers. They seem less interesting, though they're far more intriguing than the liars. Harder to catch too. Get this."

Delery leaned in.

"First you have those who tell the truth but not the whole truth. They'd be ostracized if they told everyone what they really thought all the time. It's interesting which truths they choose to tell and which they conceal. See how conniving they are?" Marais asked.

"Sure, I'm with you," Delery said, both curious and amused.

"Then you have the truth-tellers who think they're telling the truth, only they're dead wrong. In their own minds they're honorable. In actuality they're either stupid, have a limited world view, are blinded by dogma of some sort, or all the above."

Delery assented, wondering what was next.

"Those are only a couple types. Assholes all of 'em. Don't get me started on the fickle ones whose truth changes often. Give me an honest liar any day."

Delery didn't know where to go with that, so he brought up payment, they discussed it, and upfront money exchanged hands.

"Nice to meet you, Bobby Delery," Marais said.

He rose again, wincing more this time.

"Be strong. Be careful. Keep on."

"Thank you, Mr. Marais," Delery said.

"Mr. Marais?" was the sniffed reply. "Not Z.A. either. Sounds too Alpha/Omega. Call me Brotherman. Or B."

"Good luck with your writing, B. Thanks for digging up the dirt for me," Delery said while they both stood, clasped outstretched hands, and then curled their fingers in for a second shake.

Delery left not knowing whether he'd been in the presence of a madman, genius, or both.

Chapter 7

Sylvia Asbury took Galvez over to Almonaster. Spanish philanthropist Don Andres Almonaster is buried under the floor of one of the buildings he paid for, St. Louis Cathedral in Jackson Square.

Galvez Street, named for Bernardo de Galvez the Spanish governor of Louisiana in the late 18th century, became a one-way street in the opposite direction, so as usual, Sylvia made an immediate right and proceeded a block before turning left onto Miro, the one-way heading upriver. It shouldn't surprise that Miro was named after another Spanish governor, in fact, the one responsible for rebuilding the French Quarter after the Good Friday fire such that the colonial district resembles Havana and Cartagena to this day.

Sylvia was interested in New Orleans history but that of another kind when she sighed and looked over at her daughter Erykah, in town for the weekend. Both were schoolteachers who'd been illegally fired along with 7,500 others after Katrina. Sylvia had eventually gotten hired by a charter, but Erykah had moved an hour north to Baton Rouge for an available position.

Sylvia had a second job. Nothing happened in her block and the adjacent ones without her knowing about it. Almost nothing.

"You know I personally got us street signs after the storm. Claimed abandoned houses before Katrina. Squatter's rights. So I could kick drug dealers off my block. Block our family built in the 20's," she said.

"Yes, mama," said Erykah.

"Councilman gonna tell me it's none-a my business? Rob Russell gonna tell me instead of the city fixing up that club for a community center or gym, it's none-a my business why state troopers are guarding the doors 24-7?"

"No, mama. I mean yes, mama." Erykah had spent the last eight years living in the Red Stick, which had flattened the highs and lifted the lows of her New Orleans accent.

"Child, are you listening?" Sylvia asked.

"Yes, but I'm hungry. You know I get lightheaded," said Erykah.

"We're almost there, baby. See here, already turning," said Sylvia as she made a right at Elysian Fields.

"Alright, mama," said Erykah.

"Listen, it's no concern of mine what they're doing in that club? Not construction. There's history there. Billie Holiday sang there. Dave Bartholomew."

"Ray Charles, Fats Domino, Professor Longhair," added Erykah from hearing the list quite a few times.

"Oh," fussed Sylvia. "You tired-a hearing this. I used to have pictures, nice pictures of it, before Katrina. Receipts, Erykah, receipts. No more."

"I'm just hungry. That's all."

"Mmm hmm. So this historic landmark for our people gonna be nothing but a mystery. I even wrote a letter to Mr. Thalmus, the bank president who came up back here. He and his wife Judy have done a lot around the city. But this white man Russell stops taking my calls?" As an aside, she said, "You know I've got beaucoup white friends."

Erykah looked at her mother.

"Woman that's gonna interview me is white. But this is *our* history. Back in the day Club Desire was a nice place for our people to come to. You'd see groups walkin' up the block since the streetcar let out at Tonti. It saved people too, that club."

"Mama, I'm trying to forget all that," said Erykah.

"The second floor saved us. When I was little during

Hurricane Betsy. Katrina too."

"Uhhh," said Erykah, annoyed. "We should-a gone downtown. Never floods down there."

"This is our land, child. We don't leave our land," stressed Sylvia.

"Why do you care so much about a fire hazard club? Haven't even had music there since I was born," said Erykah. "Only thing it's good for is Clawfoot," she added.

"Even Clawfoot needs a place to sleep that's not the tub in Evelyn's garden. You know they're not letting that old wino sleep in the club anymore. Baby, it's been over a year. Councilman Russell wants to be the next mayor, but he can't answer a constituent?"

She threw her left hand into the air.

"Officer Thompson's a good man—you know him—but he says he can't talk about it and changes the subject. Won't even look in that direction like he's scared. How's a man that big gonna be scared less it's something shady?"

"Mama, my stomach," pleaded Erykah.

"And Herbie Berry, B-Smooth, says it's none-a his business. How come these men always in everybody's business don't wanna talk?"

Sylvia turned left onto Abundance, crossed the street after traffic passed, and pulled into a parking spot in front of a corner restaurant.

"Time to talk," she said.

When they entered, a young blond woman lit up and waved to them.

"Mmm hmm," Sylvia murmured while nodding.

Sylvia and Erykah walked over to the table midway along the right.

"Hi. I'm Kristin Kluger. We spoke on the phone," the woman said.

They exchanged pleasantries before Sylvia got to the subject at hand.

"Miss Kluger, I'm happy to talk about the club's history. New Orleans history. But I can't do that and eat at the same time. It's not polite. So how about first we eat, then we talk?"

The interviewer flashed a microexpression of annoyance, realizing she wasn't in control. She quickly recovered, though, and they all ordered, ate heartily, and chatted.

Kluger noticed that Sylvia made small talk with her mouth full but was not about to bring it up.

When at last Kluger's salad, Sylvia's Crawfish Monica, and Erykah's Stuffed Bell Pepper Plate were finished, Sylvia leaned forward to observe the notebook and pen Kluger placed on the table.

"Club Desire was the biggest and nicest in that area, but it wasn't the only one in the block. You know Frenchmen Street? All those bars and clubs and whatnot up and down a couple blocks. 2600 block of Desire was like that for black people."

Kluger was surprised. "Wait, that whole block was active with nightlife?" she asked.

"Oh, yes," Sylvia said. "Daytime too. And the blocks around it. See, there was a supermarket, doctors' offices, a few po boy joints. Plus all the bars. Other side of the canal—the project side—there was a big movie theatre. Bowling alley next to it. A bar, The Project Bar. Bynum's Pharmacy."

"Okay, wow," said Kluger while she quickly scribbled.

"Jim Crow—you know what that is?" Sylvia asked and Kluger nodded vigorously. "Back then black people had our own businesses. It was like country city there. Never saw whites, less it were men lookin' to buy drugs."

"Do you know when Club Desire was built?" asked Kluger.

"I know what my mama told me. Back in the 20's my grandfather built several houses. Right in the 2500 block-a

Desire. Round the same time, the streetcar line—you call 'em trolley, but we say streetcar—it was being built. Came up Desire and turned off at Tonti. The men building it would walk up to a little coffee shop owned by a man named Charlie Armstead."

Kluger asked Sylvia to repeat the name and she did.

"They told him it'd be good for our people to have a nice place to go for entertainment. He bought some property and eventually opened Club Desire. There's history. Billie Holiday sang there," said Sylvia, continuing through the list of notables while Erykah mouthed them in her mind from memory.

"Two floors, Miss Kluger. First floor had an elevated stage with tables and chairs surrounding it. Fit about 150 people. On the Desire Street end was a separate restaurant and long bar so a person could drink and not interfere with the concert. Upstairs had a balcony all the way around and a hotel on one long side. Mmm hmm."

"I'm stunned," interjected Kluger. "I moved here three years ago to go to Loyola and hadn't heard any of this before I saw you on the news."

"That's how it goes," said Sylvia. "I've been trying to get the city to renovate it. There was damage during Katrina, you know. Isn't even a place with a liquor license in that whole area. We call it up front, because it is to us. Not backatown."

"How long was it open?" asked Kluger.

"Club Desire opened in the 40's and closed in the 70's," said Sylvia. "Most-a the places closed up by the late 70's. People started going elsewhere after integration. Some black people think they're better if they mix with whites. There were some shootings too, especially by the gambling joints. When I was a child there was the Polka Dot, Jolly's, Ceola's, Three J's, Green Shade, and some others."

"Were they all the size of Club Desire?" asked Kluger.

"Oh, no. They all had music, though. Club Desire was

the special place. Had a phrase painted on the wall. "The Downtown Club With Uptown Ideas."

"I like that," said Kluger while she jotted it down.

"I expect you want to go on by the club. Follow us," said Sylvia.

Kluger made an odd expression. She grasped for words, turned red, and rubbed the mole on the left side of her nose.

Both Sylvia and Erykah turned their heads sidewise in curiosity.

"Are you okay, miss?" Sylvia asked.

"I'm fine," said Kluger. She was concerned about crime in the area of the Upper Ninth Ward surrounding the club and didn't want to go there. Despite preparing herself a solid ten minutes the previous day for how she'd respond to Sylvia, the subject had knocked her flat.

"Fine," she repeated. "Must've been something I ate." She steadied herself.

"Food poisoning from salad?" wondered Erykah.

"I think I should head back home and get some rest," said Kluger, speaking as though it was the first time she'd pronounced the words. "I've already found some old pictures of Club Desire. The rest of the research for my article can be done online."

Sylvia was still stunned. "You don't want to see the place I've been talking about. It's there. Only a few minutes away. Can't get in it, but that's another story."

Kluger began to resemble the red shells of the crawfish Sylvia and Erykah had eaten the day before.

"Is there a reason you don't wanna go?" asked Sylvia.

Kluger's arms swung out like a novice skier and her words tumbled out. "No, no reason at all. I said I was fine, but I'm really not. Not fine at all. I should just go home. But let me take care of your meals. The information is invaluable."

"I hope you get to feeling better, Miss Kluger. I'm sure it'll happen sooner than you think. Have a blessed day," said Sylvia while Erykah nodded in agreement.

Mother and daughter rose from their chairs in unison. Sylvia took a step to the side to shake Kluger's hand, but though the arms of the young woman were still outstretched, her head slumped down in dejection.

Sylvia and Erykah's eyebrows lifted together. They turned and left, missing the spectacle of Kristin Kluger's hands returning from their span to grasp the crown of her own head and shake it savagely.

Neither mother nor daughter spoke until they were seated back inside the car.

"What was that all about?" wondered Erykah.

"You couldn't tell?" Sylvia replied. "No way her 'lil self was going back by where I live. Wasn't gonna tell us that. I'm grown. I know."

"Mama, to be fair there are shootings back there from time to time. I worry about you by yourself. Remember when Ms. Fields across the street got her place shot up a few years back?"

"It got shot up 'cause her son who ain't shit was inside with his friends who ain't shit, and CeCe Fields doesn't care they turned her place into a trap house. Tell me people don't get shot up *all over this city*. Erykah, some people love black culture but sure don't like black people. Don't get me wrong 'cause some of 'em that feel that way are black themselves."

"If you say so," said Erykah.

"Girl, don't you get saucy. 'Less you wanna keep makin' excuses for Miss Ann in there."

Sylvia started the car, and as she backed out of the lot Erykah saw Kluger leave the restaurant, no longer disheveled. Strode in her Gucci heels with purpose and no sign of discomfort over to her car.

"Oh my goodness!" exclaimed Erykah. "Mama, you were right. She's not sick."

"Of course your mama's right," scoffed Sylvia.

"Why didn't you call her out?" asked Erykah.

"Child, I don't have time to call out every bullshit ass lie." She showed a shark smile, all teeth and intention. "I do it just enough to keep me young."

"You got that," agreed Erykah.

While they were heading home and Kluger was on the way to her Warehouse District condo, two unlikely carfellows had finally figured out the object of their search.

"Yes! I'm making' moves. Winning. Hear me?"

Leon Sparks was overjoyed that his closed eyes childhood game had paid off. He picked his nose with panache in celebration. It was a cartilage scraper.

"That's gotta be it. Turned left, street was smooth, then bumpy. I had you keep going straight. Can't be obvious. Size-a that building's gotta be right. Two floors. Guards outside. Trooper guards no less. Shit," he said.

"Do you want me to loop back around and go by it again? Make sure?" asked Grange.

"Hell no. Tip 'em off? No, I'm lackin' right now. What I got at home ain't heavy enough. No, Morris. We goin' back to the Capri. Get some firepower. Tomorrow's Easter, but come Monday after dark we comin' back."

"I did my job," protested Grange. "You don't need me anymore."

"Yes I do, Morris. We wait it out 'til Monday night. I'm gonna get my vengeance. You part-a this. Drive."

Grange reluctantly continued on from Florida Avenue, where he'd been idling with the canal on his right and abandoned fire station on his left. Around the corner one block back sat the building where Sparks was certain he'd been held.

That block was mostly vacant lots. Several buildings had been torn down in the years following Hurricane Katrina. Only a couple houses and a beauty salon were standing and occupied.

The only structure of any stature remained as it had for decades, though now covered with graffiti. All of its interior and exterior architectural touches stripped.

No sign, no stage, no long bar, no ironwork, no tables and chairs, no beds and nightstands upstairs. Faded phrase on the inside wall. The crowds and glory days were long gone. Performers had moved on, most of them dead or retired.

It remained as a reminder to almost no one but a few. It was a box, a hull, an eyesore, a historic snore to everyone else. The better known Dew Drop Inn also hobbled along Uptown, but most others of its type were long gone.

Leon Sparks was fixated on the building that remained on the lakeside corner of Law and Desire. It meant no more than vengeance to him, but in its heyday it was Club Desire.

Not many years before the club opened, the city extended basic sewerage and water lines to that part of the Ninth Ward. Until then it had been a muddy flood-prone area peopled by working class blacks and new white immigrants from Europe, all of them mostly neglected by the city.

Present day, those blocks around Law and Desire made Leon Sparks and Morris Grange think the same way as many in the city did a century before, of a desolate isolated backwater.

This was in contrast to parts of New Orleans where newcomers seemed to arrive every day with cash in hand to throw at property in particular areas. Sharp contrast.

Chapter 8

Detective Nelson Harrell yawned deeply. Reached over and lifted his cup of coffee. The burger and fries were next. Typically he ate two fast food meals a day in his car. Not ideal but came with the job.

He'd managed three and a half hours sleep at best, been up and out until 4 a.m., and after some down time, was on his way back to the office, which in this case was the street. Hadn't been out late enjoying himself. Was paying the bills by working a detail for a swanky Uptown party.

Details were the off-the-clock jobs that everyone in NOPD liked to pick up to augment their low wages. As part of the consent decree with the feds, the city ran the program, though with the dysfunctionality in which most everything else operated. Of course they took a cut.

Harrell licked the ketchup from his moustache. He'd grown one, closely cropped, since returning to civilian life after three tours as a Marine. Each tour was eight months, with a year in between, and he'd returned to New Orleans a seasoned twenty-five year old in 2006.

He'd been stationed in Asia and hadn't seen combat. His work continued at home when he helped get his parents back in their Gentilly home post-Katrina and bought the one across the street for himself.

His military background got him recruited by NOPD where he ended up finishing near the top of his training class. After a few years as a rookie officer, he'd been promoted to robbery detective. His clear rate brought him to the attention of Detective Sergeant Ellison who eventually plucked him for the elite group of Homicide Detectives.

He was going on his second year in the position. There were twenty-two other detectives, which was at least a third low. Homicide division wasn't immune from the alarming attrition rate NOPD was experiencing.

"Maybe when I get older I'll get on cold cases," Harrell said to his French fries as he shoved two into his waiting mouth. "Mostly guys with wife and kids who want 9-to-5 and no weekends," he added.

It was 10:15 on a Saturday night, and he'd had to leave the couch. His turn was next in the rotation. That's how it worked.

"It's gonna turn even quicker just in time for summer," he realized to himself, thinking about the expected uptick. Plus, rumor had it they'd be losing Clarence Reid and Joe Thornton in the next few months. Both vets.

"That'll probably put me on nine cases this year," he said aloud. "What'd I have last year? Seven?"

Though the number didn't seem like much, the accumulation of investigation, evidence, and court time added up to make for quite a crunch if working beyond six cases annually.

He didn't have far to drive. "The vic was shot in front of the stop light at the end of the exit from 610 to St. Bernard Avenue," dispatch had told him twelve minutes before.

Harrell yawned once again, turned left from Mirabeau onto St. Bernard, and finished his coffee. Plenty of traffic out as expected on a Saturday night.

"Need to cut out the fast food," he said, tapping his stomach with his left palm. "I got love for you, invested in you a lot, but you gotta go," he said to his belly.

Harrell had tried a vegetarian diet in the last year, other than the meals he ate in his car. He'd been one step from also giving up beer. Hadn't had much time on his hands lately, and when he wasn't working both regular and detail jobs, he was too exhausted to jog in City Park.

As he approached the scene, he saw that I-610 had been at street level when the vic exited, requiring no ramp, only veering off to the right. I-610 rose after the exit and was elevated above St. Bernard.

Harrell could see cones set up so that exiting drivers were kept to the left of the two lanes, meaning the vic must've been about to turn right onto St. Bernard rather than left.

All the usual suspects were there. NOPD reporting officer, his commander, EMS, coroner, and crime scene technician. Harrell's job was troubling to his soul, but he took pride in bringing justice to a crime-riddled city, as much as one man could. A few of the others on the force called him "boy scout," but Harrell liked being a man who helped his community.

He knew the white shirts played favorites and how bad they would burn anyone they wanted to, but he felt a responsibility.

Did he like that he got painted with the "lazy and corrupt" brush because too many of his colleagues were indeed both, keeping their palms out and working harder to keep from reports than doing their actual jobs? No, but for the time being he could deal with the b.s. from the city and know that those who knew respected him.

"Boy scout, pssssh. Here we go," he said while parking in the blocked off part of St. Bernard.

Harrell stepped from his car and surveyed the scene lit up for nighttime. Not what he expected.

"Hey, Calvin. You the first one here?" he asked the officer charged with protecting the scene.

"No, Pearson was," said the officer, pointing out the broad-shouldered redhead closer to the focal point. "Check out that silver ride. Porsche 911 convertible. Pretty. Was pretty."

Harrell's gaze hadn't left the car mentioned since he left his own. The luxury vehicle was set back a car and a half length distance from the traffic lights. Rectangular windshield support was mostly empty of glass and bent on the driver's side. Hood was dotted with bullet holes.

"Rolling solo?" he asked, seeing it was a sleek two-seater.

Officer Calvin Campbell replied. "Yeah, unless a passenger got away. Damn lucky if they did. This looks like a chopper," he said, meaning the street term for an AK-47.

"Someone definitely heard that kind-a noise," mused Harrell. He moved closer.

The crime scene tech was busy with her camera and evidence cones in front and to the side of the car. She nodded at Harrell.

"Yvonne, was this a shootout?" he asked.

"I've found nothing but identical casings. Up to forty-seven that all came from the same gun. The shooter used two magazines," she replied. "There was a pistol under the driver's seat, but he hadn't had a chance to grab it.

"So this all happened from the front, obviously," said Harrell. "Probably at the red light. The Porsche driver?"

"Dead," she said. "You know…" She waited for him to finish.

"I'm with you," he said. "Déjà vu from that Broad Street shooting over a year ago. And those others. The one Diaz was working before Christmas and one Harper had last summer."

"Right," she affirmed.

"Who was the vic?" he asked.

"A Gerald Turner. Heard of him?"

Harrell's eyes widened and head tilted back.

"Yvonne, I know two Gerald Turners," he said. "One's a two-time felon working as a line cook over on St Charles by Napoleon. Takes the bus. The other Turner kept his nose clean all this time, but everybody knew he was deep in it. G-Nice got hit, huh?"

"Whoever it was made sure the job got done like those others," she said.

"Competition? I'd heard he was into dealing guns, drugs,

and women. Even Medicare fraud. City's on this whole gang homicide thing with the feds, though, going for RICO conspiracy charges on the high profile cases. Turner was doing his business without bloodshed, so we weren't after him," said Harrell.

"How's that match up with the other vics?" she asked.

"Nothing but good words from everyone I interviewed about the guy killed on Broad. Definitely nothing pointed to why he and his family got it. I'd have to double-check with Diaz and Harper, but I'm pretty sure their cases were like Turner. Not social, not out there too much, but doing real well flying solo in the underground economy."

"Underground economy," she said with derision. "The money's underground. The killing never is." She returned to her work.

Harrell knew that Yvonne Verrett's little sister Jamilah wasn't a day over sixteen when she was fatally shot while out with her older boyfriend. They'd come upon a group who'd been beefing with Donde.

Harrell felt it as much as anyone could, whether at the crime scenes with family members and neighbors or doing interviews afterward. He never promised he'd find the killer, only said that his heart went out to them and he'd do his best.

"Alright, Yvonne," said Harrell, and he walked over to a man alongside the car.

"Detective," said Officer Tim Pearson. "I'd shake, but look at my fucking gloves," he added while tilting his head to his dirty hands. He had a spray of freckles across his nose and cheeks

"Anything DNA-wise point to the shooter?" asked Harrell.

"Not a thing. Somebody wanted this dude wet. They picked a good spot too. Look around, no cameras," he said as Harrell instinctively turned.

"Good point," said Harrell. "A planned spot, chosen, not

random. The highway's a buffer. These trees are a buffer." He looked at the green wall planted along the riverside of the exit lane. "The only possible witnesses were moving past too quickly to see much, unless they were exiting behind this Porsche."

"If somebody was idling behind the car when it started getting shot up, I'll bet they put it in reverse and got the hell away," said Pearson.

Staying focused, Harrell asked, "Got his phone? In case any calls of note."

Technology had been of major benefit to the Homicide Detectives. Perps posted court admissible photos of guilt on social media. Cell phones could be tracked to specific locations. Cameras were beginning to proliferate.

"Yes, sir. Got it. Bagged it," Pearson replied.

Harrell was aware of his name being called. Officer Campbell was standing with two people.

The detective turned and walked back toward St. Bernard. Traffic was moving slowly because of all the rubbernecking.

"Detective Harrell, these people saw something," announced Campbell.

They all greeted each other. She was wearing a nice dress of 80's vintage while he sported a suit and tie of a few more decades prior.

"Detective, we were driving past, Harold and I, on our way to bingo. He hadn't won in a while. We were hoping for better luck," she said.

"You had to work that in, didn't you?" scolded the old man.

"Well, it's true. You thought your luck was changing after that good omen and we…"

"Marian, are you going to tell everyone about my fortune cookie?" he snapped.

"Ma'am, what did you see here?" asked Harrell.

"Well…" She looked peeved at her husband. "I was driving

because someone wanted to reread something he'd gotten inside his cookie at dinner." She pointed to the other side of St. Bernard.

"We were going that way, so when we passed by here and heard the noise, I automatically turned," she said.

"Yes, keep going. What kind of vehicle was at the light?" asked Harrell.

"A van," she said. "A plain white van. Nothing fancy. At first I wondered why it wasn't driving to get away because the sound was so loud. The noise boomed like it was everywhere. I immediately drove faster. When we got further past—we were probably under 610—I could see smoke and the gun sticking out."

"Sticking out of where?" asked Harrell. "You didn't see the shooter?"

"No, only the end of the gun sticking out the back of the van," she said.

"The doors were open?" asked Harrell.

"That's not what she said," piped up the bingo player. "You're not listening."

"Harold!" she chided. "The gun must've been shooting from out a back window. No doors were open. I just saw the end of the gun keep shooting at the poor man in that car," she said, pointing at the Porsche.

"Ma'am could you see the driver?" asked Harrell. "To know it was a man?"

"No, but isn't it always," she said matter-of-fact. "Couldn't see the driver of the van either. It's dark out, even with the lights."

"Anything else?" asked Harrell.

"No, that's it. I should drive Harold back to church for his game. He complained the whole way back here, don't you know. I made him leave bingo because it was the right thing to do."

"Shut up, Marian!" snapped the old man.

"Thank you both," said Harrell.

The couple had barely left when a news van pulled up. First media arrival.

"Not a word about what the witnesses saw," Harrell stressed to Campbell who was firmly positioned on the public side of the police tape.

The officer grinned wryly. "She's fine, but don't worry. 'Fuck outta here' is the only thing they're gonna get from this brother."

Before Harrell could turn, out popped WWL reporter Terri Green who called to him the second her feet touched the pavement.

"Detective! What happened here? Name of the victim?" She used her words to allow her to bridge the gap while she jogged up to Harrell. The cameraman who'd been driving followed her as quickly as he could manage.

"Miss Green, come on. You know better. We're collecting evidence. Once the vic's family is notified you'll be the first to know."

"Along with everyone else." She wasn't in the habit of giving up so easily. "That's a nice car. High profile person?"

Harrell shrugged and turned up his palms. "I've got work to do."

"Detective, can we talk about this over coffee when you're done?"

"Miss Green..."

"Terri," she pushed.

"Terri, I'm heading to Broadmoor for a detail once I leave here. You'll get the press release as soon as it's ready. Have a good night."

He turned to face the damaged car and the rest of his colleagues but said loudly enough for her to hear, "I'll take a rain check on the coffee."

On the other side of the Fair Grounds, two men were in a produce warehouse that contained no food, only a beat-up sedan and a certain white van. It was three minutes before 11 p.m.

One of the men was wrapping an assault rifle in a small rug. When he finished, he walked over and shoved it behind a human-sized stack of pallets.

His partner was on the phone.

"Nobody saw nothin'. Just a couple cars drivin' past. Subject was definitely taken care of."

"Good work," said the man on the other end of the line. "I've been following it on the scanner. Sounds like it was clean. Nobody behind the subject when you both exited?"

"Nope. Fourth time worked. Knew he'd eventually exit there. Perfect like a fuckin' rainbow."

The man in the warehouse was dressed in black, a solidly built character in his early 70's. He'd worked in the casino business over twenty years. New Orleans, Las Vegas, Brooklyn. A few other endeavors too, like the present one.

His head was a little large for his body. It looked particularly stretched what with his long forehead and graying pompadour.

"Rainbow, huh? Rainbow for the city. One less vermin," came the reply from up near the lake.

The speaker loosened his tie and looked from the leather couch he was sitting on over to the person behind an imposing desk. Approval was given by a tilt of the head.

"You both'll get paid the usual way. Make sure you're not seen leaving."

"Got it, boss," said the man in the warehouse.

Shortly after, he and his partner left the space on the corner of Maurepas and Crete in Mid City for a drive in the sedan across the river to their separate abodes in Gretna.

The other two men were in a book and liquor lined home

office in Lakeview. The door was closed.

"Damnit, but Turner had to go. Now we need another source of revenue. The new guy Sparks will help, but we have to identify someone else," said the man behind the desk.

He was clean cut, barely to age forty, and had the strong scent of arrogance.

"Yes, sir," came the reply from the couch.

"Ultimately I'm helping this city. Exterminate all the drug dealers as far as I'm concerned. But Kevin, we must build up my war chest if I'm gonna have a snowball's chance at being mayor in 2018."

"You're right," said Kevin Warren as he tapped on the couch. "Turner reneged on the deal. He had to go. Plus, holding those criminals back in the Ninth Ward makes the city safer. Gets them off the street. They're all investing in New Orleans, especially those we let walk free. Like a tax."

Chapter 9

The day known as Easter Sunday began for many with Mass or an outdoor sunrise service in one of the many New Orleans cemeteries.

The cities of the dead numbered over forty, almost as common in a neighborhood as a corner market or bar. Unique for the U.S., the tombs were above ground, which some attribute to the high water table, others to tradition.

Because of the cozy relationship with the dead, a religious service, much less a meal, in a cemetery isn't an odd or morbid occurrence whatsoever. No more peculiar than any other routine.

So many people away from home for the morning is also a bonanza that goes beyond the preachers' haul. Thieves are a little less furtive when they march from door to door.

Everyone else was asleep until crawling into Sunday like any other Sunday. Late.

Almost everyone. Bobby Delery wasn't an early riser but neither did he waste the day.

He'd met Ellis for Saturday dinner at Cochon. Didn't have much to update her about beyond his meeting with Z.A. Marais. She'd told him how her gymnastics students were doing.

Delery was feeling hollow enough to only want to return home alone after the meal. He'd worked some aggression out with his barbells before drinking himself to sleep again.

This time he'd put away his records before nodding off. *Man-Child* by Herbie Hancock, *So Many Rivers* by Bobby Womack, and *Barzakh* by Anouar Brahem.

It was a small step of improvement, which counted for

something in his mind, but barely since he couldn't see the top of the deep well he felt trapped in.

By midmorning on Sunday he'd kept to schedule and went over to the gym. In the commons area on the St. Claude side of the Healing Center building, he'd seen and heard a man in a wheelchair holding court for a few young people.

Delery had recognized him as Griot Sam. Hard to miss the man in his tortoise-shell glasses and goatee who always had something to say from the seat of his wheelchair.

He'd been finishing up when Delery had come upon the group.

"I've told you how our people started civilization, but look at us now. White man has raggedy shoes on his feet but money in the bank. We come correct, but all we got is what we're wearing or driving? We should be owners, not just buyers. Okay, enough from me."

Griot Sam and Delery had seen each other at the same time.

Delery had spoken first. "Yes, sir," he said.

The old man had narrowed his eyes and thrust out a bent index finger.

"You, you're one of us."

Delery had locked eyes and nodded, impressed but not surprised that the wise Griot Sam had figured him for a black man at a glance, despite his appearance.

"Don't forget it," Griot Sam said firmly.

Delery was thinking about the exchange a few hours later after finishing a lunch of leftovers. Continuing the linkage made him turn to thoughts of his family.

Everyone had been cremated. No ashes. No grave markers. Nothing but his memories.

"I'll make it up to you," he said to the room around him, as if Isaac and Curtis were there listening.

"I'm sorry to both of you. You too, Mama, but I'm gonna

make this right."

Significantly, he left his dad out of the one-sided conversation, which was cut short by the ringing of his phone.

"Bobby, it's Tiny. How're you doing?"

"Best as can be, man. Real shaken up, you know. Thanks for putting me onto Brotherman."

"Of course. I don't know what he'll find, but be cautious. It's real out there."

"I hear you," said Delery

"How's B doing?" asked Tiny.

"Seemed fine. Must've twisted his ankle, though."

"Right good chance he did. Man walks absolutely everywhere. No car. No bus. He started doing that when his wife died. Totally unexpected. Little disease with a big name got her. He was one of the good guys with NOPD, but he quit that. Owns a little real estate and helps people out. Bet I know how he twisted that ankle."

"Didn't you say he walked everywhere?"

"Well, yes," said Tiny. "Walking. But B has a system. He sees a different lady each day of the week. My cousin LaTonya used to be Tuesday until she moved to Houston to make real money in the oil business."

"Wait. He has seven women that he only sees on specific days?"

"Correct. No side piece thing. Listen, the man had a love and he lost her. Now he's got *arrangements*. Can't call him wrong for that. They all know the terms. Nobody gets tired of each other. I'll cosign for B all day. Time for me to go, Bobby. Got to prepare for court."

Delery paused a moment. "Court, Tiny?"

"Didn't I mention? I'm an attorney. 90% of these cases never make it to court, but you never know. Can't have a Monday case sneak up on me."

"Okay, thanks for checking up, Tiny."

"Holla at you, Bobby. Knuckle up but be careful, hear?"

Delery decided to take a walk and get some fresh air. He headed upriver on Dauphine and barely crossed the train tracks when his phone rang again.

"Bobby Delery, zebra man. Good afternoon. I've got information."

Delery paused before remembering the comment from the day before and knew it was Z.A. Marais. "Hey, how're you doing? You got word already, B?"

"I'm sitting on two of the three pieces of information you requested. Names and reps," Marais replied. "Need to grab a pen?"

"I'm outside," said Delery. "But I won't forget."

"If you say so. Two men here, fairly similar. Military backgrounds. Only word is that both are stand-up and solid. In fact, I used to be on the force, so I know one of them. This guy worked both murder cases. Your brother Curtis. Isaac and his family too," he said.

Delery felt a surging anticipation.

"Brother's name is Nelson Harrell. Two r's. Two l's. I knew him as an officer, but it's no surprise he was bumped to Homicide," said Marais.

"And the parole officer?" asked Delery. He heard the train's horn and saw it about to crawl across St. Claude, eventually to block him from his side of the neighborhood, so he reversed back across the tracks.

While his back was turned as he proceeded on Dauphine, he completely missed the spectacle at Chartres and Press. Three armed men inside a car parked sideways in the street.

When a couple vehicles arrived at the roadblock, two of the men jumped out of their car and each commandeered a vehicle at gunpoint, leaving three people standing in the middle of

Chartres. Two were stunned. One was merely annoyed.

Delery neither saw nor heard any of the dual carjacking, engrossed as he was in Brotherman's reply.

"The parole officer who handled Curtis was Bernard Tackett. Fairly new guy, but he's good people. Both he and Harrell are as honorable as anyone could be. Your only problem is…"

"What?" interrupted Delery.

"Parole officers' case loads are high, plus they can't officially tell you a thing other than public info. There *are* ways around that, of course. Pretty much the same with a Homicide Detective. You know, some of them are working the equivalent of two full-time jobs?"

"Thank you, B," said Delery. "And that third piece of information?"

"Still working at it. Keep on," said Marais.

"You too, sir," replied Delery.

He was a full two blocks away from the train tracks. A couple in their early 20's, recently moved from Connecticut, were waiting for the 911 dispatcher to answer their call about a stolen electric car.

Near them, a slightly older man dressed far more casually was filling in his employer Land of 1,000 Bikes, which was located just outside of the French Quarter.

"Jessie, I just got jacked by the tracks. Both me and another car. I'd packed the van with eighteen bikes from the warehouse like you wanted. I'll make sure the cops fill out a report so you're covered for insurance. Change the locks. They got my keys. Dunno how long it'll take. I'll walk back when it's done."

After listening to his boss curse wildly, Earl Matassa hung up and walked over to sit on the steps of NOCCA's newly renovated art gallery and restaurant building. The classroom buildings of the high school for the arts stood on the opposite side of Chartres.

"That's some bad fuckin' luck," he said. "They take the damn magnets with the store's name off each side, and it's just a regular lookin' white van."

Matassa looked around and called out to the couple still standing in the middle of the street as if to mark the spot of the crime.

"911 answer yet?" he yelled.

"No!" called one of the women. "This is unacceptable in a modern city."

"Yeah, well," said Matassa. He lit up a joint to get a smoke in the meantime.

Across town at the Capri Motel, Morris Grange was also in need of his usual to take the edge off. "Come on, Leon," he pleaded from the chair inside room 138. "It's been almost two days."

Leon Sparks was sprawled across the bed watching TV. He picked up the remote and threw it at Grange, hitting the younger man directly on the right cheekbone.

"Shut your trap or I'll break you up. You think I play?"

He stood up quickly, wiped the side of his nose twice with his knuckle, and walked over to where Grange was bent, rubbing his cheek.

Sparks leaned over so closely his girth was an inch from pressing against Grange.

"I don't play. Hear me?" said Sparks.

Grange began to whimper. "Not my fault. I don't know why..."

"Answer me, Morris. Do you hear me?" thundered Sparks.

"Yes, I hear you," said Grange with a bleating tone void of inflection.

"You better. I don't fuckin' play."

Sparks walked to the door. "Gotta do some business on the phone. I'll be outside. Stay put."

Making sure he had the room key card, he stepped outside and firmly closed the door. He was wearing only a white undershirt and black dress pants.

"Gotdamn if this meth head gonna keep tryin' me," he muttered.

Flipping through the names in his phone, he turned to the left and moved off to the side of the building. Looked above to make sure no one was on the balcony to listen in.

His A+ Used Cars office manager answered from home on the second ring. "Yes?"

"Davida, it's Leon," said Sparks.

"I know that. How many years have we worked together?"

"Too many," he said. "Kiddin', Davida. Listen, I've got somethin' to deal with, so not expectin' to be on the lot 'til Tuesday. Maybe Wednesday."

"Alright, Leon," she said.

"Work the phone for me. Darryl should have plenty-a product. He shows up needin' more, watch him when he takes it. And sell a car or two, Davida," he said.

"Of course I know all that. Have a blessed day, Leon."

He hung up, saw the time was 3:22 p.m., and was fully aware that Davida Wallace knew what to do.

"Davida might could keep runnin' the drug thing if somethin' happens to me Monday night," he thought. "Long as she don't know that. Bet she does. Probably too old to care anyway."

"Where you at, youngblood?" he asked right off in the second call.

"Waitin' room at the hospital," was the reply.

"What? You fucked up my money, Darryl?" pressed Sparks.

"Nosir nosir," said Sparks' drug runner Darryl. "It's all good. Somethin' else. My cousin Rabbit got crawfish juice in his eye. He in the emergency room right now."

"Y'all dummies trippin'. Flush his eye with water. Don't you know nothin'?" stormed Sparks.

"We looked up symptoms for burst appendix so they take him in. Right now Rabbit tellin' 'em he all cleared up 'cept a burnin' eye. That way they take care-a him," explained Darryl.

"You motherfucker, you," said Sparks. "Better not be wearin' them weed man socks neither."

"Nosir," said Darryl adamantly while he looked down at the socks in question.

Sparks sighed, guessing he was hearing no more than a line.

"Listen up. Ms. Davida gonna be workin' the phone for a couple-a days. She calls, you jump. Hear me? Should have plenty-a product, but go by the car lot you need more. No matter what, you bring me my money on Wednesday."

"Yessir," said Darryl in a way to both show respect to his boss and toughness to his girlfriend sitting next to him. "D-Love get it done," he added only for her.

"What you say?" puzzled Sparks as he held the phone away from his body like it was infectious.

He continued, "Just do your damn job!" and hung up.

Sparks picked his nose with a free pinky.

"D-Love get it done," he grumbled while putting his phone away.

When he entered the motel room, a thought crossed his mind. He quickly walked over to his shoes and socks underneath his casually tossed shirt.

Sparks reached inside his left black-and-brown shoe, retrieved Grange's car keys, and put them into his back pants pocket.

"Dumb ass," he spat across the room, disgusted that he'd left the keys there and Grange hadn't thought to pocket them during the outside phone calls.

"What did I do?" warbled Grange.

As Sparks dressed himself to go back outside for errands, he couldn't resist.

"Looks like some whitesploitation you're watchin'. Didn't think you supported that, Captain Obvious."

"Leon, treat me like some kind of freak. I can take it. Say whatever you want, but lots of people agree with me. We've had enough of the reverse treatment. You just don't see who the real victims are," asserted Grange.

"Mmm hmm," said Sparks while struggling with the last shirt button across his belly. "Gotdamn if I thought I'd see the day. Put your shoes on 'fore I slap the shit outta you."

Sparks had figured that the $1,000 he'd tucked under his spare tire in the trunk was enough for them to arm themselves, but he wanted to make sure. They were on their way to withdraw the maximum $500 from an ATM and pick up some food along the way.

"When we get back, Morris, it's artillery time. Ready up for tomorrow night. Might let you get a little fix too," said Sparks.

As they were leaving the parking lot, Grange looked around puzzled. "I wonder why there are there so many Tennessee license plates?"

This was a subject right in the heart of Leon Sparks' area of knowledge, and it jolted him from his doldrums at being cooped up in a motel room.

"Memphis pimps. Bringin' sweet honey down the river. Matter fact, after I get what's mine, after you help me get my retaliation, Leon Sparks gonna have himself a smorgasbord-a Memphis honey."

Chapter 10

Ellis Smith made it to Bobby Delery's apartment on Dauphine at 5:20 p.m. She had groceries in tow and a notion to drag him out of his deep well.

"I'm not doing this alone," she told him right off, referring to her famed twenty-five clove garlic chicken. "You've got some chopping to do."

An old adage says a person's eyes are the windows to the soul. In the case of Ellis the shutters were drawn. Not that she was distant or unfriendly, merely elusive and often unreadable.

Her eyes also seemed cautionary to Delery; something had happened in her past that still hurt deeply. "Maybe she has her own family issues," he thought while they walked from room to room as was often the case to arrive in the kitchen of a shotgun house.

Her keen intelligence and sense of understanding often outmatched his own. He knew that all too well. She was beyond her years.

"My head's been so into this whole family thing, it's like I'm seeing her with fresh eyes," Delery said to himself. She struck him with as much force of her spirit as she had when they first met at the bookshop on Chartres.

It doesn't overstate things to say that if the fashion and advertising industry suddenly became less limited and myopic in how they regarded beauty, women like Ellis would be on magazine covers and billboards the next day.

She was stunningly attractive by any standard but the one with the most public influence. Ellis didn't have a silhouette like a ruler. The lady had hips. Wasn't pale as a dove's tail.

Ellis also wasn't one to lower the bar of expectations for

others, particularly Delery, though she truly felt for everything he was going through. She was a woman of few words, so when she spoke it mattered.

She waited until the groceries were on the counter.

"I'm from here too, Bobby. I know why people choose to carry out justice on their own instead of letting Tulane & Broad handle it. You with me?"

He agreed without speaking.

"I know you're hurting. I also know you're not gonna stop until you find out who killed your brothers. You're a smart guy. But you…"

She got choked with emotion.

"You have to do this by the book. You're not a killer. I mean…I hope you don't have it in you to do that," she said, waiting for an answer.

Insomnia had made him jittery. He held his left hand in his right to steady himself.

"Ellis, I don't even have a gun. What am I gonna do, strangle somebody? In my position—it's not fair—but in my position I come in contact with a lot of law enforcement people."

She nodded lightly as he continued.

"What I'm saying is it's not fair that different people get different justice. But…I may not be a rich man. I may not be a white man. But I'm definitely gonna use my criminologist job to get justice."

"Just be…," said Ellis.

"Hold on a second," he interrupted. "Let me tell you my plans. I'm taking tomorrow off from classes. Meeting with Curtis' parole officer and the detective who handled Curtis and Isaac's murders. "

"That sounds reasonable," she said. "You scared me when you confronted the man outside Captain Sal's. Bobby, I can't live every minute worrying if that's the day something bad happens to you. I can't. I won't."

Delery took her hands, realizing he was about to tell the truth by exclusion, exactly the way Z.A. Marais had described it. Emphasize certain truths while leaving others out.

"Ellis, I know the Homicide Detectives in this city are good. People have no idea how good. But often with a case, things shake out and change over time. Friends become enemies. A woman tells on her old boyfriend. This is important to me, but so are you. I'll be careful," he said.

She'd been studying him while he spoke. With an accompanying nod, she squeezed his hands.

"How about we go to another room before we start dinner?" asked Delery.

"Another room?"

He tilted his head back.

"Are you sure?" asked Ellis.

He leaned forward and they kissed.

Initially Ellis was hesitant, thinking Delery wasn't ready, but as she let her dress fall to the hardwood floor, she could see he was thirsty for her.

Ellis intuited that since things had been happening *to* him, he needed to feel like a man in control of his life. She let him guide the way, knowing she'd get her turn soon enough.

Clothes strewn. Piling.

Eyes fixed. Yearning.

Hips flexed. Craving.

No words. Learning.

Primal. Knowing.

Arms legging.

Legs arming.

Alternating, quicker, pleading, quicker.

Shadowplaying.

Together.

When they finished, their bodies fell into the interlocked curl they'd grown accustomed to. His right arm around her waist. Her left holding it in place.

"I needed that," he whispered.

"I know," she said with her eyes.

After a few minutes passed, they dressed and returned to the kitchen, ready to make dinner. Delery took the food out of the grocery bag. "Chicken, garlic, herbs, sweet potatoes, white wine, broccoli, long grain brown rice, rosemary, and parsley," he thought as he saw each item.

He turned, stepped back, and held her hands. "I love you," he said, realizing those three words sufficed. Instead of him explaining the third entity the two of them automatically created. Instead of several things.

Definitely instead of saying, "I'm tired and feel like shit, so the fact that you love me makes me feel like somebody."

"I love you too, Bobby," she said, thinking they were feeling a flow of emotion because they'd just been intimate and had that sweet release.

All that was also true, the tangible and the abstract wrapped up into three words. The universal shorthand of a couple.

The idea of harm coming to Delery was still foremost in Ellis' thoughts. "People die every day in New Orleans. Would if they were better shots. I don't want him messing with those who think life is cheap."

Ellis didn't want to express that aloud, but she did mention that which her train of thought next led to.

"Bobby, did you read about the shooting last night at a 610 exit? Right at St. Bernard?" she asked.

Delery was focused on chopping garlic. "No. Haven't been paying attention to news the last few days," he said.

She continued. "It happened at the exit stoplight. Someone in a white van shot up the guy in the car behind."

He put down the paring knife. "Say that again."

"A guy in a nice car was behind a white van at the St. Bernard exit of 610. He got shot. Sprayed with bullets, it sounded like," said Ellis.

"Wow," said Delery. He repeated it while he breezed by her.

"Bobby, what're you doing? We need to brown the garlic."

"It's gonna have to wait," he said while walking briskly up front to his desk and computer.

A few minutes later he returned to the kitchen.

"Listen to this," he said.

"Bobby."

"The garlic can wait a minute. I found the news story you were talking about. Here's the thing. Violent crime has its own typologies, its own predictors. Strain theory, previous exposure to violence, revenge…"

"In English," she said. He'd heard this before.

"Most New Orleans street crime is mayhem. Sloppy, whether instrumental or expressive," he said.

She gave him the look.

"What I'm trying to say is that this shooting sounds similar to the one that killed Isaac and his family. Tiny said there were no witnesses that came forward. I don't know if there was a white van. Regardless, Isaac's shooting probably wasn't random. This one either."

Ellis put the baking dish of sweet potatoes in the oven. "Bobby, I think you're wanting immediate answers. The perfect puzzle piece to have it all match up. I remember another shooting at a stop light last November or December. It happens. Terrible, but it happens."

"Wait a minute. There was another one? Ellis, trust me on this. Shootings at stop lights from the vehicle in front are uncommon. They suggest motive, premeditation, and stalking. There's way more effort involved in this than a couple guys beefin'," said Delery.

She remained skeptical. "You really think so?"

"Ellis, criminology's what I do," he stressed. "Look at it this way. We all have ways we do things, patterns of behavior, places we like to eat, where we put our toothbrush, that sort of thing. So do criminals. They put signatures on how they do things. Like I said before, a lot of New Orleans crime is just messy. But for somebody who knows what he's doing, like a hit man, there's a definite signature. It doesn't vary much."

"You think it was a hit man?" she asked.

"Who knows, but I think it was a hit. According to the news, the detective working the St. Bernard shooting is the same one I'm planning to meet tomorrow. Nelson Harrell's his name."

Nelson Harrell himself was at that moment making his way into NOPD headquarters. He'd had seven hours of sleep, the most he'd seen for the past month, so he was feeling good. Liking the flexibility to do a little Sunday night work.

Right after a killing was the time to dive into it. People more willing to talk. Fresh in everybody's minds. Might prevent the retaliation.

"How's the crotch?" was yelled out from behind the main desk, breaking Harrell's train of thought.

"Excuse me?" he said, more than a little puzzled.

"You know, New Orleans. The crotch of the South," said the man standing next to the receptionist Paulette.

Like a child showing off, he kept going for her sake. "The sweaty, stinky, nasty, hinky crotch. Our fucking city."

"Whatever you say," replied Harrell diplomatically. He was aware that Chris Rizzuto, the officer standing before him, preferred cozying up to Paulette than service calls and reports.

Rizzuto turned a little more serious. "You got number forty-three, huh?"

"Sure did," replied Harrell on his way past.

"Gonna put us way past last year's 150 by the end of the year. Wasn't like this when my people—Sicilians—ran things. Very little killing. Man could walk down the street at night and make it home safe," said the officer.

Harrell stopped. He had a minute. No more.

"The king of crime in New Orleans? Everybody's just gonna lay down and say, 'Okay, he's running things, so I'll stop and pay tribute?' Of course not. There'd be more bloodshed than now. And who'd be the kingmaker? You? Me? The Chief? Vaccaro? Maybe you're meaning to legalize it all?"

"No, no, no, no, no," said Rizzuto. "I'm not talking bullshit like legalizing drugs. Fuck, we legalize weed, they deal H. Already are. Legalize H, they deal coke and crack. Legalize all that, they deal some synthetic shit that doesn't exist yet. Even so, legalize it all and Tyrone's still gonna shoot Jermaine for looking at him funny."

Harrell lifted his lower teeth over his upper lip and covered it all with his lower lip. It was his way to literally hold his tongue and keep himself in check. Kept it there a long five seconds.

"I mean if...," started Rizzuto.

"No, you said your piece. *My* turn," snapped Harrell. "Officer," he began, dangling the title before continuing. "Half the black men in this city don't have jobs. Paycheck jobs. Probably a good number of that half with jobs are being underpaid and working two or three of them just to get by. Do I want people *dying* in my city? Obviously not. Do I *understand* that people will do what they have to do to put food on the table? That too many men are in situations where they end up lashing out? Yes. They commit violence, degrade themselves, all sorts of low things. Look at the big picture. I've got work to do."

Harrell passed by on the way to his desk.

Rizzuto shrugged. "Fuck outta here," he said, as much to

save face in front of Paulette as Harrell.

Nelson Harrell shook his head at the tossed-off comment behind him. "Lord, keep me strong from fools." He'd expected the officer was going to naively bring up that some in the black community didn't report crime because they didn't care or profited from it.

"He'll hit me with that next time," thought Harrell. He knew when it came up he'd cite a few past examples of citizens who were not so mysteriously killed after talking to officers. Couldn't be that a few of our brothers and sisters in blue tipped off their gangbanger friends, business associates, or cousins, could it?

"Trust is key. It's everything. No rapport, no trust. No trust, mouths stay zipped up like mine initially was back there with bonehead," he thought, remembering his father's strict command to 'Zip your lip!' the few times young Harrell got mouthy. He'd take that over the backhand that most of his friends got.

As Harrell sat at his desk, he saw a couple messages left for him. Neither for last night's shooting, though. Before he went home for the night, he wanted to put together the list of TBI's, people To Be Interviewed, starting Monday. Also pull potentially related case files.

He looked at his calendar for the week. No detail job for Sunday through Tuesday. One Wednesday. Then long days— probably 9 a.m. to 9 p.m.—from Thursday to Sunday working NOLA Fest directly with the staff. That meant he'd be doing regular police work overnight, sleeping three hours if he was lucky.

"I need to get through the interviews for the Gerald Turner case before Thursday if I can," he said softly.

Harrell figured if he saw a strong enough connection between his new vic, Ed Diaz's from late 2014, and Morgan

Harper's from a few months before that, he'd take his findings to Detective Sergeant Ellison.

"Maybe the Delery cases fit in too. Odd ones. Can't overreach on it, but if I can figure out the connection, the through line, Ellison might give me one of the cold case guys to assist," he thought on his way to the file room.

"Through line. I like that. Common line running through the cases to make sense out of it all. Same as a spine. That's what I'm looking for, to see if these cases fit on the same spine."

Harrell knew with the Homicide Section being understaffed and overworked his boss wouldn't take to time-wasting flights of fancy. If he could show solid spine for the stoplight murders, that meant a chance at improving the clear rate in one fell swoop. Probably commendation too.

He looked down at the beginning Turner file on his desk before heading toward the file room.

Harrell wondered what NOPD would look like in five years. The attrition rate was largely those in blue on the streets. White shirts who hadn't seen the far side of a desk in years were going nowhere. Overstaffed and underworked. Twice as many as needed.

"Yet they barely train anyone or provide oversight. Easier to train by discipline," he groused before reminding himself not to wade into negativity.

"You might not get out of that quicksand, Nelson," he said to himself.

Harrell found the folders for Diaz's cold case vic Willie Broadus and Harper's Michael Price where they were supposed to be. Also grabbed the two Delery case files. Ten minutes later he was back at his desk, engrossed.

An hour later he came up for air and looked all around him in wonder, his skin tingling.

"Turner, Broadus, and Price are essentially the same man.

Small business owners in their 50's. Thought to be involved in the drug trade. Money makers. Shot and killed by AK-47. Second car back at a stop light. No drivers behind them as witnesses," he said as he read the words jotted down on his notepad.

"Turner at 610/St. Bernard, Broadus at Carrollton/Bienville, Price at Orleans/Miro. And Isaac Delery at Broad/Bayou Road. Lotta guys get shot, but this all smells like the same thing. How does Curtis Delery's death fit on the spine?"

Harrell was in the flow. He worked through his thought process with an active left hand. Tapped the chair legs like a hyper teenager. Pencil hovered in anticipation. He knew what was next.

"A witness who had a green light yielded for a white van speeding through the intersection right after he heard multiple gunshots on the scene where Broadus was killed," he said. "Here we go."

Chapter 11

Truth be told, Leon Sparks' tough guy persona was fairly recent, following in line with his emergence in the drug trade. He'd been a reclusive nerd before but had come to think of himself as nothing less than a stone cold badass.

His casual and smooth car salesman side still had its moments, though. As necessity on the lot. Also when charm was a better tactic than aggression. Even when he was a buyer.

"You tell me," he said to the sixteen year old standing on the other side of the bed. "I wanna leave here with firepower in my hands and cash in your pocket. Two of us need to deal with a handful of men. Maybe more. I think we're lookin' for military type shit, but what do you advise?"

The teenager known as G.P. nodded. He looked like he was dressed in a high school uniform minus the all-black shoes, though he'd dropped out two years before.

G.P.'s clothes hung off his lanky frame. He was the definition of the physical type known as an ectomorph. All lines and angles.

His assistants, friends who were only there for added presence, were of the other two body types. One had a muscular physique. He was the mesomorph. The other was rounder than Sparks and would be more so by the time he finished the two-liter cold drink in his hand. He was the endomorph.

It was as if a physiology textbook was opened before Sparks and Grange.

"I do have some expertise on the matter," said G.P. with a certain diction that surprised the buyers.

He stepped to the bed and pulled back the covers to reveal an array of weaponry.

"Burner time. What you see at the foot of the bed are Glocks. Trustworthy and well made. Light. Easy to conceal."

Sparks was pleasantly surprised that parking lot chatter had led him to G.P. The kid could sell water to the ocean.

"This one here," the teenager pointed, "and the one next to it. That's a Glock 27 and a 19. I call them Jay and Beyonce. Bey holds fifteen in the magazine plus one in the chamber. Nine plus one capacity for Jay, but he's the more powerful option."

"These," he said, anticipating Sparks' next question, "are what you use when you want to take care of a little business. Or protection. Emphasis on little. Do you know what I mean?"

Sparks nodded. "I see where you're going with this," he agreed. "We'd have that element of surprise at first but limited when we really need to turn up."

"Right," smiled G.P. as he pointed at Sparks.

"I like you, man. All business. No bullshit." He tapped his chest with his palm. "We're simpatico."

"Definitely, G.P.," said Sparks, realizing he needed to use the kid's name more and wishing he could hire him on the spot.

"Well…," said the teenager. "That leads us up the bed. I've seen your boy eyeballing these from the get go. Am I wrong? What do you go by?"

This was an attempt by G.P. to bring Grange out of his shell so the seller could suss out what the sole white man in the room was about. Sparks had impressed upon Grange before they arrived that his mouth needed to stay shut, but before the older man could speak, Grange did.

He'd been standing stunned with a facial expression like an imbecile. Couldn't believe how differently Sparks was acting. Definitely couldn't believe that the two men were conducting illegal business with the civility as if they were in a board room.

Only thing that kept Grange from completely bugging out, the only bit of normalcy he was experiencing, were the noises from the rooms around them.

From the room below, he could hear the staccato grunts and moans of a couple rutting like there was no tomorrow. In the Capri, that might be right.

From the room on his left, two women were violently yelling at each other. Every name in the book and then some. "No, *you* get the fuck away from *me*, you stinkin' ho-nose."

From the room on his right, an agitated man was desperately railing against both the inadequacies and conspiracies he perceived in the world. "I know you're watching me. I see all your eyes. Why won't you help me?"

Having spent enough time in the motel, all this was oddly normal and expected by Grange. It calmed him and brought back focus that he needed the 8-ball.

The brief silence in the room before Grange spoke made G.P. and Sparks hate him, for by the surrounding chaos they were reminded that their own propriety was a sham. The curtain had fallen revealing the two were as coarse as those surrounding them.

G.P.'s two friends remained scowling as they'd been instructed. They only stood there as mesomorph and endomorph, because after their dark skin color those shapes were how they were praised or mocked, vilified or celebrated. Whether snap decisions or ongoing opinions, the shape of their shells was the be-all and end-all of high school.

Meso and endo joined G.P. and Sparks in curiosity about what Grange would say.

"I'm Morris Grange," he bleated. "You have all these guns, but got any meth?"

G.P.'s grudge against Grange was amplified by the comments. He raised his voice. "Are you that stupid? Don't tell me your full name. This motel is crawling with dealers. Do I look like I push meth?"

Sparks for his part stared at Grange. "Damn, Morris," was all he could articulate, realizing he needed his partner intact for Monday night.

G.P. began to pace alongside the bed in agitation.

The change in climate bothered Sparks. He'd figured that none of the guns were loaded but was starting to wonder.

The screaming, yelling, and thrashing about from the other rooms stopped for a few seconds. In that time, both G.P. and Sparks became men of action.

G.P. yelled, "Out!" at Grange while Sparks leaned back and slapped his partner across the face. Before entering the room, Sparks had dug into his nostrils with the two key fingers of his right hand, and the dried mucus stuck fast to Grange's cheek with the crack of impact.

Grange's head spun to his left. He tipped over and fell to the floor, knocked unconscious. Meso and endo's eyes popped. They each expelled one loud punctuating laugh like air rapidly leaving a balloon.

Looking at the prone body with disgust, Sparks said, "Only thing he should go by is punkass. It's better anyway. Let us grown folks do business."

The two men gave each other almost imperceptible nods. G.P. said, "Alright," and Sparks responded with, "Alright, alright."

They were ready to continue, but the mesomorph had kept his alpha male self at bay for as long as he could stand.

"Wait. You sayin' I ain't grown?" he threw at Sparks.

It was G.P.'s turn to deal with a mouthy partner. "You dumb motherfucker. What I tell you before?"

Meso shrugged, uncomfortable with being chastised.

"You know what I said. 'Be in the space but know your place.' Shut your bad remembering ass up. I don't want to check you again."

Meso looked down at his Timbs.

G.P. took a deep breath.

"Things of this nature happen. Right here right now the only two who gonna express themselves are my man here." He gestured at Sparks. "And me."

"With you on that. No more fussin'," said Sparks. "You were workin' up past the Glocks."

"Yes sir," said G.P. "If you're looking to light it up, these are probably more to your liking. First one here is the AR-15."

He lifted the long gun and handed it to Sparks.

"See how good that feels. Don't worry, it's empty. This carbine here doesn't only look good. You hear more about the chopper, the AK-47, but reality is the AR-15 is more accurate, has better range, same size magazine. That's not just me talking."

"If all that's the case," said Sparks thinking out loud, "then it costs more, huh?"

"You need to look at effectiveness. What will help you get the job done. Price tag's nothing but a number."

"It may be, but what kind of numbers are we talkin'?" asked Sparks while he handed back the weapon.

"Good news. It's deal day. You can walk away with this AR-15 for $350. Less than half price and brand new." G.P. gently returned it to the bed. "The AK-47 next to it'll cost you $200. I've got two each of those."

"Alright," said Sparks, calculating in his head. "And the Glocks?"

"The 27 is $250. $150 for the 19. You can see I've got a bunch."

The weapons spread out across the bed had been stolen from a gunshop in Kenner the night before, so G.P. was looking to sell. At the same time, he knew they'd go quickly without having to give them away.

"I'm thinkin' about two of these. Serial numbers filed off?" asked Sparks.

"I didn't file the numbers off because once you use them, I assume you'll get rid of them, if you know what I mean," said G.P.

"Got it," said Sparks, understanding completely.

"A man with a decision. Let me sweeten the pot. You buy three, at least two of the big ones and the ammo too, and I'll throw in an emergency light. One of those strobes to put on the dash. Roll up with that thing flashing, no more waiting in traffic. Or have people think you're NOPD, it that's advantageous."

"I'll take you up on that. AR-15 for me. Glock 27 back-up. The AK-47 and 19 for this fool," Sparks said, looking down at Grange who was starting to stir. "Much kickback with the chopper?"

"There's definitely some recoil," said G.P.

"Punkass here is gonna have to deal with it, then," said Sparks. "Gotdamn if he ain't a mess, but he's gonna learn."

A few minutes later, Sparks and Grange walked along the balcony, down a few stairs, and across the parking lot back to their room. Sparks' arms were full and his pocket was lighter. Grange had a bruise in a mélange of purple, blue, and red.

"Morris, I'm gonna make it up to you," said Sparks, not wanting to listen to Grange for the rest of the night and most of Monday. "After I drop this off, we're gonna get you high. That'll help with the pain."

Grange looked straight ahead. Speechless and holding a grudge.

"Cat got your tongue?"

"It hurts to move my damn mouth, Leon. You happy?" warbled Grange angrily.

"Then don't make me go upside your head again," said Sparks.

After stashing the guns, ammo, and emergency light in the closet and throwing the bed cover over it all, they returned to the parking lot. It was oddly empty, which led both men to believe the creatures of the night were lurking in the shadows.

Luckily they had no more than to step out onto the Tulane sidewalk to find that the entrepreneurs were out and parading their wares for the benefit of traffic.

They bypassed the miniskirts and tight jeans for the first drug dealer they saw. He looked angry and half strung out on his own product.

"What it do?" he asked Sparks.

"Not for me," Sparks replied and hooked his thumb toward Grange. "Got meth?"

The dealer smacked his thigh three times. "Mu'fuckin' meth. Ain't that predictable."

"I told him," said Sparks with an edge in his molasses-voice. "Captain Obvious, I said."

"None-a that shit," said the dealer. His red eyes and scowl made him look like a wolf in search of prey. "Got something else that get ya goin'."

"What's that?" grimaced Grange.

"Click-em," smiled the dealer with his teeth. "A big J with embalming fluid. Shit'll fuck you up."

"What the hell? No, Leon. That'll kill me. Where's T-Eddie?" spat out Grange.

Sparks smirked. "Don't want too much 'llucinatin' and paranoid shit from him. We take an eighth…nah, I'll be generous. Make it a quarter. You got rollin' papers?"

The dealer's eyes sparked as he gestured them off of the sidewalk and back to the shadows.

As they followed him, Sparks said to Grange, "Emblaming's just a term. Not like the stuff used in a funeral home. It's PCP liquid sprayed on weed. You can smoke a joint, right?"

A short way upriver from Tulane Avenue's first block downtown, Kevin Warren was driving Councilman Rob Russell. Warren, Russell's Chief of Staff, looked over to the left when they crossed Perdido. "That'll be your house in a few years. There you go."

"Damn well better be," said Russell. His father was businessman and developer Rivers Russell. Immediately upon Rob graduating with his MBA from Harvard the elder Russell started his son off with a few riverfront parking lots in the French Quarter and the order to, "Make more money from them. That's your first test."

The parking lot contract was a political patronage thank you from then mayor Antoine Augustine. Rob Russell succeeded, was given a few real estate parcels to manage, and a decade's worth of further responsibilities. Eventually his father felt comfortable enough to see the benefit in financially propping up his own blood over anyone else.

Russell easily won the City Council District C seat at age thirty-five, beating a former judge who'd spent more time on vacation than on the bench. The district included the cash cow Quarter; adjacent neighborhoods Treme, Marigny, and Bywater; as well as Algiers, the only part of Orleans Parish across the river.

The father/son pact soured, however, when father was caught in bed with his son's wife Jacqueline while a baker's dozen of father's friends sat around the room watching, cheering, and sipping vintage Chateau Mouton Rothschild. They were equally amused by Rob Russell's fury.

Midway through his first term, Russell angrily swore to his father that he was a self-made man who needed no more money or assistance of any kind. Problem was that to be mayor someone had to pay for it. Most of those who'd be happy to play kingmaker and contribute to Rivers' kid's mayoral run were the men observing in the bedroom.

Russell and Warren had concocted a unique alternate financing plan.

Both of them noticed two men at the edge of Duncan Plaza, adjacent to City Hall. One was gesturing to the other. Like a blur, the tell-tale crack and flash of gunfire came from both of them. Neither seemed to be hit as they ran in opposite directions.

"Rob?" asked Warren, slowing down. "Want me to stop and call it in?"

"What's the use? They're already gone. 911's probably backed up with over fifty calls for this district alone. Steps from City Hall," said Russell.

"Pretty bad," agreed Warren as he continued on Loyola past the Main Library.

"It's on Walter Vaccaro," said Russell, referring to the mayor. "There's barely NOPD presence anymore. Too shorthanded for the pro-active task forces much less regular patrols."

"Exactly."

Russell continued. "And you know what? If we didn't have a couple dozen thugs in our holding cells right now, they'd be terrorizing or killing innocent people. It helps the mayor big time."

"Speaking of," said Warren, "we've got five of them who now say they can come up with the money for release."

"Kevin, see if we can up that to at least ten. By the way, what'd your scouting turn up?"

"I found a building down across the Industrial Canal at Dorgenois and Lamanche. No neighbors around. Just empty lots with tall weeds."

"Good. Roof's okay?" asked Russell.

"The space will work," replied Warren.

"I suppose no balcony, though, for guys to get hung by their ankles and realize we mean business," mused Russell.

"No balcony. We leave the deserted club behind, we leave the balcony. Our men can all be there Monday night to move operations. The van will be transporting the criminals. I rented a U-Haul 26-footer for the, uh, holding cells. It's simple. Won't be any sign we were there."

"I hate we have to do it, but Sylvia Asbury has a big mouth. She sounded suspicious enough in her last voice mail that she might bring attention to the space. Can't have that. Damn busybody," said Russell.

"Pain in the ass who doesn't realize we're making her neighborhood safer," said Warren.

"I guess the move was going to happen anyway, what with the fire station returning and the city about to start covering the Florida Canal. Couldn't be our base forever. The new spots's good, you say?"

Warren nodded. "Good as it gets. As far as safety, if a couple state troopers, a handful of cops, and a pair of made men can't get handcuffed guys down to the Lower Ninth Ward, who can?"

"Also," said Russell, thinking on the fly. "If it so happens that any of them have to be…taken care of, make sure cuffs are removed before dumping the body."

"Don't worry. It'll be handled. You're not going to be there?" asked Warren.

"Sure, I'll be on hand. But you…," Russell pointed sternly at Warren. "You make damn sure the area is clear. Secured perimeter. That whole thing."

"I will, but sir, you have to cover your face in case a random person walks by. That was the problem a year ago when we were setting up the operation, remember?"

"Kevin, you don't need to tell me what to do. I handle goals and strategies. You carry out objectives and tactics.

Plus, have you forgotten? A *junkie* saw me and the cages. The kind of person who shits himself and gives head to stay high. Eliminating him was no loss to society."

Warren chose his words carefully. "True, but remember we also had to take care of the junkie's brother and family. My guys saw the brothers talking. No other choice, but we ended up, uh, eliminating a couple kids in the process."

"Do you think I fucking wanted that, Kevin?" yelled Russell. "The goddamn junkie saw me! Saw my face! Saw in the club! Your people couldn't catch him. Took a fucking day to find him. Yes, there was an unfortunate situation to deal with. You tell me. What the hell was I supposed to do?"

"I know," said Warren. "Please cover your face this time in case of a surprise, even if you keep your distance."

"Don't worry about me," fumed Russell. "You worry about a new source of revenue. More dealers. More criminals. None of this is worth anything if it's not bringing in money. Endgame, Kevin, remember. Mayor Rob Russell in 2018."

"I'll work on that Tuesday once the move's all complete." Warren said.

Russell huffed and scratched his face, which looked lacquered from constant tanning sessions.

Warren, whose own complexion was that of a brand new eraser, proceeded on Claiborne. They passed a parade of cabs dropping off angry people at the impound lot. Towing based on the most minor of infractions, along with an increase in fees and tickets, was a hallmark of the Vaccaro administration.

Chapter 12

It was a quarter after nine Monday morning when Bobby Delery drove past Lafayette Square.

It reminded him of the park a block from the apartment where he grew up in Fort Wayne, but not because of any similarities. McMillen Park was where he learned to play baseball when he cared about baseball. It was where he learned to ice skate, indoors during winter, when he slightly cared about ice skating. He never cared about golf, so most of McMillen wasn't for him.

McMillen was over eighty times larger than Lafayette Square. If there was any commonality it was green grass interfering on the holy urban trinity of asphalt, concrete, and exhaust. The park only made him think of the other one because his dad George was in his thoughts.

"All those years," Delery mouthed aloud. "He probably never sent my letters. Made me think Mama and my brothers didn't care about me. The man acted like a snake."

He'd sworn a few nights before that the news wasn't going to break him, only heighten resolve to find whoever killed his brothers.

"I owe you all that much. To find out who took away my family. No way I'm gonna let this go. Not gonna do you like that. I'll solve this," he vowed as he pulled into a metered parking spot.

Delery hadn't yet had reason to visit the Orleans Parish Parole Office but expected it to be like all the others, and in that he was correct.

Lots of signage. As clinical as the DMV but with the ability to put you back behind bars. The receptionist looked like she'd seen and heard it all.

Time to start using his job title. After signing in, he announced himself as, "Robert Delery, Tulane Criminologist, for Bernard Tackett."

He sat for over ten minutes before a man stepped into the waiting room and called his name. Delery sized him up. Armed and had handcuffs on his belt. Louisiana-shaped badge next to the gun. Looked in shape.

Delery passed through the metal detector and met him at the doorway. They shook hands while walking back to the third office on the left.

"What can I do for you, Mr. Delery?" the man asked.

"You're Bernard Tackett?" Delery wondered before seeing the nameplate perched on the desk. "Yes, you are. I'm here about my brother."

"So, you're not here in an official capacity," said Tackett with rising tension in his voice.

"No sir. I was away for years and recently found out my brother Curtis was killed. I thought maybe you'd have information that would be useful. Here, let me grab my license to prove who I am."

Tackett sighed and scratched his trim beard. "That won't be necessary," he said. "Dunno how useful this is, but all I can legally provide you is what's publicly available whether he's your brother or not. Also, I've got a huge caseload, so I don't really have time."

"Mr. Tackett, I only need a few minutes. I'm sure that in my position I can help you out some day," said Delery.

"Curtis Delery was your brother, huh?" asked Tackett. "I guess in this instance it'd be fine since he was killed. Let me pull his file, and I'll summarize the terms of his parole. Any applicable narratives too. Sorry, notes to us."

After a few keystrokes, Tackett said, "Okay, Curtis Reginald

Delery. This won't help much. You probably know he liked the H. Got caught after burning a house down. That was his second time in. Two-time drug felon. We placed him at maximum supervision. I'm so damn busy now, though, and he never showed a tendency toward violence. Probably would've drop him to a lower level if he was still around and stayed clean."

He paused. "Sorry, man. I didn't mean it like that. We're just real clinical here. Not always p.c."

"No offense taken," replied Delery. "What does maximum supervision mean?"

"That's monthly. Alternating OV's and PC's. Office Visits and Personal Contact, as in I go to him. Curtis was staying in a little apartment back by Almonaster. Our last meeting was a few weeks before his death."

He stopped to chew his gum a bit and continued in a ho-hum voice. "Ten minute meeting. No drug screening. I was way behind on those. He was coming here in a few months, though, and wasn't looking real good. As in, I'm guessing he was back using."

Tackett turned and looked at Delery. "Requirement of his parole. Pass the drug screen or go right back to prison.

Delery's eyes hardened as he remembered what Tiny had told him.

"Mr. Tackett, the way Curtis was killed...do you know if he was a C.I.?"

"Never came up. Nobody from NOPD ever called about him or mentioned it, but who knows. Whew, it was grim. They don't just shoot him, they pound a nail in his tongue. Looks like he was doing a little talking, doesn't it? You know, Mr. Delery..."

Tackett gestured with left palm up then right, alternating a few times as if weighing the odds of two paths.

"I got a voice mail the night Curtis was killed."

"What'd he say?" pushed Delery.

"Five words. Well, six. He always called me Tack. His message was, 'Tack, saw him at the club.' That was it. Six words, some commotion, that's it. I told the detective about the message. Tried the number back, but no answer by that point."

"Nothing more?" asked Delery. "Anything?"

"Not at all," said Tackett. "I assumed it must've been a guy Curtis was beefing with. Maybe an old drug buddy."

"Could be, but then why kill Isaac and his family too?" Delery thought out loud.

"Oh, man. I knew a family got shot up that same night, but I'm so busy. All them were your family? That's messed up."

Delery nodded. "I know. That's why I'm here."

"At the same time, Mr. Delery, realize who you're dealing with. When I go out serving warrants, it's a group of us. Four in the morning, bulletproof vests, heavily armed, the whole deal. That's my training. Playing Rambo's not for everyone."

"Agreed," said Delery. "But my brothers aren't going out like that."

Fifteen minutes or so later Delery parked a block from OPP, Orleans Parish Prison, a little further from the main police headquarters. When he entered he announced himself with his job and affiliation as before.

This time he barely waited a minute before the receptionist called out, "You can head on back."

He nodded before walking through the doorway and down the hallway. When he got to the main area of desks he paused.

He hadn't met Homicide Detective Nelson Harrell before, so he wasn't sure how to proceed. A right arm stretched up in greeting across the room, so Delery walked that way, a ship toward a lighthouse.

The first thing about Harrell that struck Delery was Harrell's reflexive expression, a smile. Vice versa Harrell noticed how haggard Delery looked, but that was typical in his line of work.

"Detective," Delery said with outstretched hand.

"Professor," Harrell replied while shaking.

"Oh, have you been in one of my trainings?" Delery asked.

"No. I've seen you around, but I was in the midst of a high-profile case each time. Since the training was voluntary… another time." He added diplomatically, "I heard good things, though."

"Yeah, sure you did. The egghead's here again kind of things," said Delery.

"No, it's all good." Harrell turned serious. "I didn't know your name. Your last name. You aren't related to…?"

He didn't want to complete the question if he didn't have to. Harrell was typically a man who spoke in a low key but declarative way, though he occasionally went automatically ambiguous.

"My brothers are—well were—Isaac and Curtis Delery. They were both killed the same night over a year ago. Isaac's wife and kids too," said Delery.

"Shoot. I had a feeling you were about to say that."

Harrell tapped a stack of folders on his desk. "Those are cold cases now. Normally I wouldn't deal with them, but they're sitting right here."

"Because of the 610/St. Bernard shooting?" asked Delery.

Harrell initially showed surprise before acknowledging, "Maybe so. But something else comes to mind. Where were you when your brothers were killed? I would've interviewed you then, but your name never came up."

"I've been away for years. Parents split up."

"Let me ask you now. You didn't have any contact with your brothers all this time? Nothing to add that might help?" asked Harrell, wondering about any sort of drug dealing Isaac Delery might have discreetly been wrapped up in.

"I wish I did, Detective Harrell, believe me. That's why I'm here, though," said Delery.

"Call me Nelson," said Harrell. "I'll admit I'm looking through the Delery files and a few other stoplight murders over the past year. You know not to put too much stock in easy answers."

Delery looked hopeful. "But the more there are, the more likely a pattern shows itself. Except for Curtis. His doesn't fit, but it's got to be connected. It was too bizarre."

"I agree with you on that. The nail—that wasn't random," said Harrell, leaving out that neither Delery murder seemed to fit with his general theory.

"Was Curtis a C.I. that you know of?" asked Delery.

Harrell nodded, following the logic.

"There's no sign of that, though the nail definitely speaks to a point being made about talking. Weird thing—one of my own C.I.'s said right after the death that he started hearing rumors that Curtis was one, though he'd never heard it before. But again, nothing on my side of things shows that."

Delery leaned back. He was exhausted and trying to keep it together.

"Did any witnesses see a white van around the time of the other shootings?" he asked.

"Professor, I..."

"Call me Bobby. Please."

"Bobby, I can't start going into the intricacies of all the cases with you. You're lucky to catch me, in fact. I've got TBI's to talk to today."

"Nelson, please. Was a white van seen?" Delery tried, on the verge of pleading.

Harrell looked at him squarely. "Yes, with one of the cases, but we can't run before we start walking, if you know what I mean."

"That's something to go on," said Delery. He bobbed his head. "Anything helps."

"True," agreed Harrell. "Bobby, as a professional courtesy, I'm going to save you the question."

He leaned over, pulled out two folders, and handed them to Delery.

"The two Delery case files. I need to grab a cup of coffee and use the head. You've got until I'm back to look through these."

"Thank you," said Delery. He was truly touched.

"You may want to avoid the photos," advised Harrell as he rose from his chair.

Delery dived into the files, Curtis' first. He relived everything Tiny had told him, only with far more graphic detail. The death of Curtis Delery was quantified. The five bullets that riddled his body. The length of the nail that pierced his tongue after death.

Delery's horror continued as he gutted it out through the file on Isaac and his family. It was all as expected, but no less nauseating for it. Delery skimmed along, conscious of his time constraint, until he came to a piece of information Tiny hadn't mentioned.

He was still staring at the sentences when Harrell returned.

"Nelson, Isaac was found spun around, facing the back seat," said Delery.

"Right," said Harrell with a soothing voice. "He was probably trying to protect the kids."

"After that it says he wrote 'Law |' with his own blood on the side of the seat."

"I know, but for the life of me, I can't figure it out. I'm sorry, Bobby, but I've got to leave. Let me give you my card, so you can get ahold of me directly should anything come up. Be careful. Leave this to me. I'm on it," said Harrell.

They shook and Delery found himself more confused and distraught than he'd been since Friday.

Closer back toward Bobby Delery's neighborhood, a solid eleven sunburned members of the U-Lock Bike Gang were waking up with coffee at a café on St. Claude. Those who worked were evening shift bartenders, cooks, or ran deliveries. The others would soon start drinking the day away.

The founder and leader of the gang was a burly bearded fellow known as Nat, less of a mouthful than his given name Nathaniel Merryweather Birch. Nat was a New Englander who'd lived in New Orleans since the late '90's.

For years he was no more than a drunk adept at little beyond running through an increasingly depressing series of lovers and shabby apartments. In this he was similar to several New Orleanians.

The event that broke his inertia should be put into context. There had been bike thieves as long as there had been bikes in New Orleans. Typically the usual scraggly zombie-eyed skeleton looking for a hit. 2015 was different.

Cop shortage. Moneyed transplants. More bikes. Expensive bikes. Thieves noticing. Easy targets.

When Nat's own modestly priced bicycle was stolen outside the Lower Garden District watering hole where he bartended, he had an hour and a half walk home downriver. Like the subject of the Italian movie *The Bicycle Thief* who won't be able to keep his job if he can't find his stolen transportation, Nat became obsessed.

Friends of his also had their rides snatched in the midst of the epidemic. One drunken evening after Nat had spent his tip money for the week on a new bike, it all came into focus.

A misspent blurry adulthood edged out of his mind while he looked at his ramshackle friends and their bikes locked up outside with any manner of cable locks that had the strength of string.

Like Moses returning with the tablets, Nat's soul was stirred and he'd muttered, "I've got the answer." He'd grabbed a marker and wrote all his ideas along his left arm and across his torso.

The words and arcane symbols across the body of Nat were the crux of the U-Lock Bike Gang. They would use social media to report stolen bikes and catch the thieves. Encourage use of better locks. Travel in a pack when possible as a show of strength. Teach the thieves a lesson from time to time.

Nat threw himself into all of it with even more energy than he'd expended on maintaining lethargy. Followers or detractors, he didn't care. His mission was clear.

Nat and his cohorts were meeting to discuss their plan of action for the next few days.

"Land of 1,000 Bikes got robbed. Their delivery van was carjacked yesterday. Jessie's offering a reward. Here's what we…Gilbert! Are you fucking listening?!" yelled Nat.

Gilbert, an elfin creature with a beard longer than most and shorts shorter than all, mumbled "Sorry" in a woodsy-nymph-dancing-with-a-lute kind of way.

Nat continued. "Geez. Listen up, people. We're looking for a white van. They might have all the bikes or maybe just a few of them left to sell. Bianchi's. The expensive ones. Might also be driving around looking for more bikes. If we find the van, we find the bikes. Got it?"

As the group nodded, piercings jangled, tattoos twitched, and eyes sparkled.

One member piped up. "Nat, can I hit Treme to be closer to work?"

"Sure, Elysium," said Nat gruffly.

After he assigned the rest a particular neighborhood or sector, he looked around at each of them, jabbing an index finger bent to the side from too many fights.

"You know the drill. Comb your areas. See a white van that might be it—don't be stupid and bother delivery drivers—post your location. If you're convinced it's the one, then do whatever you can. Get the license plate number. Slash the tires. Bust up their windows with your U-lock. Anything to make it easier to ID the van if it gets away," said Nat.

The group nodded in unison. An appendage shot up, spearing the circled silence.

"What is it, Window?" asked Nat, apprehensive and annoyed but trying not to completely show it.

Though Window received his nickname for an unconventional preference of entering by windows rather than doors, he'd also never veered away from raising his hand for permission before asking a question. A perpetual schoolboy. He croaked out queries that tended to be labyrinthine hypotheticals. Window had graduated from M.I.T. and played the harp beautifully, but his power grid had a few outages.

"What if the van's another color, like cobalt, but I can see a trace amount of white in spots? Should I question when the van was painted or assume there's no point in asking since they won't answer accurately? What if I ask them indirectly?" He blushed. "Sorry, that was a few questions."

"It's alright, Window," sighed Nat. "The van will be white. These are crackheads who aren't taking the trouble to paint a van. Just find it and alert us."

"Thanks, Nat," said Window with a deep tone that didn't match his gangly elastic way about the world.

Chapter 13

When Bobby Delery returned to his car, he sat inside with the door open until he could feel his legs again. Smacked palms against knees. Eyes pierced. Lips pursed and moved in thought.

He called Z.A. Marais, anxious for an update. No answer. He hung up rather than leaving a message.

Delery took Broad home, slowing near the intersection where Bayou Road crossed. The spot where his brother Isaac and family were killed.

His eyes twitched a bit. "No feelings. Not today," he said in a voice barely above a whisper.

Delery gulped, continued downriver, and being off-kilter, turned toward the river on Elysian Fields instead of continuing on the overpass.

"Damn it. Not in the mood to get caught by a train," he grumbled.

He hadn't joined the likes of Jackson Square soothsayers and palm readers in claiming to predict the future. It was only the harsh reality of probability. When he turned onto St. Claude, he only traveled a few blocks before seeing a line of cars.

He hoped the sheer amount of waiting vehicles probably meant the tracks would clear soon enough. Plus he didn't want to backtrack.

While Delery waited, he glanced around. A mix of fancy, blight, and that indicative of a changing neighborhood. Fewer storefronts that didn't look last occupied decades ago.

Next, two handfuls of bicycles were walked to the sidewalk. Delery saw a lowrider, a couple tall bikes, a tricycle, unicycle, and other bikes not tricked-out.

He saw the earnest faces of the bicyclists, watched them

form a circular shape, and puzzled at why they all lifted up their front tires together. They followed that by dropping their bikes to the ground, punctuating the move with assorted yelling. A few fists raised to the sky, as well.

Delery noticed that other drivers in front of him were also watching as the group took cigarette packs from socks, bra's, and the pockets of both jean jackets and shorts. The furious tapping of the packs against palms, legs, and chests resonated over the slow steady clip-clop of the train finally moving.

Five minutes later, he gave himself one last glance at the smoke cloud above the bicyclists before continuing on.

Delery didn't know what coaxed a particular memory into the foreground of his thoughts like a weed stretching up after heavy rain. He was in school. 6th grade. He'd been writing his mama and brothers weekly with no response.

"I was in my room, ready to start a letter. It hit me. Why? They didn't love me anymore. Hadn't replied at all. I wadded up the paper, threw it away, squeezed my hands, and wished they were dead," he said.

Delery didn't think his one-time childhood wish had the power to make the deaths happen, but he wished he'd never thought it.

His eyes twitched as before. "I'm sorry. I didn't know. Makes sense now why Dad always said he mailed at work. He probably threw them away to make me hate you. Break the connection," he said.

Delery was consumed with his thoughts and startled when Z.A. Marais called him back with the last piece of information sought. The conversation hummed in Delery's ears while he wrote three things.

"Delery, I found one of your brother Curtis' friends. And when I say friend, get what I mean. The dude was scared of his own shadow but even more of your brother's. Not just because he was strung out. Apparently, the night they came to get Curtis, this guy was hiding under the bed. Claimed your brother hadn't mentioned anything to him about why somebody was trying to get him," said Marais.

"He didn't know anything?" asked Delery.

One word. He said he could hear Curtis on the phone but couldn't understand what was being said. The door got kicked in and no more talking, only your brother crying out as they took him."

"B, what's the word?" asked Delery, sounding jittery.

"I'm getting to it," steadied Marais. "When he was sure the place was clear, he crawled out from under the bed. Needed something for his nerves. Said he knew Curtis used the tracks under the table—you know, the tracks to add more leaves and make it bigger—to hide the stash. So, he's crouched down there. Sees a butcher knife off to the side. Your brother must've used it to try to defend himself. First thing he sees before the drugs was one word. Curtis had carved it five or six times on the underside of the table with that knife."

"What was it?" asked Delery.

"I don't know what it means, but 'Desire' was the word. Capital 'D.' Your brother chose one word. The phone was gone, so no idea who Curtis called."

"That's a good question," Delery said, not letting on that he knew Curtis' call was to his parole officer. "All he wrote was 'Desire,' huh?"

"Yes, sir. That's what this guy saw."

Marais cleared his throat. "My work is done. I've fulfilled the terms of our agreement."

"Of course," Delery assented. "I'll be by next week with the rest of the payment. Can I ask you one last question?"

"Sure, what's that?" wondered Marais.

"Did my name come up at all with Curtis'…uh…friend?"

tried Delery.

Marais mellowed his tone. "No, I'm sorry to say it didn't."

Delery sunk, though he expected that response. "Alright, thanks."

"Keep on, Bobby Delery," said Marais to close out the call.

As he'd been replaying the call in his head, Delery stared at the words on the paper in front of him.

Desire.

Saw him at the club.

Law |.

"Does any of this mean a thing, or is it no more than gibberish?" he said to his empty room.

"Did Isaac mean 'the law won' or didn't he get to finish the rest? Did Curtis mean his desire for getting high caused all this?"

Delery spent the rest of the afternoon and early evening with those and other questions worming through his conscious and subconscious mind. The words grasped hands, broke and changed places, recreating the chain over and over again.

Meanwhile at the Capri Motel, Leon Sparks was keeping Morris Grange in line. They'd just returned from Sparks using most of his remaining money to buy fresh clothes for the evening. He had a new suit, a bowler hat, and gators. All purple.

"I told you Morris, once you came off-a that high, your fool head was gonna stay straight until we go out and do our business. My vengeance. Think I want you shootin' me in the ass 'cause you all fucked up? If I can wait to slide up next to some females for a few hours, you can get your mind right," said Sparks.

"But Leon…" bleated Grange from the corner of the room where he was coming out of his bliss.

"No but's," thundered Sparks, his right fist striking the bed, bouncing the guns he'd laid out next to where he was stretched out. "Don't bring it up again."

"Okay," dribbled from the side of Grange's mouth.

"Yeah," smirked Sparks. "Here's what's gonna happen. Once nightfall comes—and I'm talkin' serious as shit dark, not no almost there dusk—then we roll in *my whip*. You get this," he said pointing to the AK-47. "And this here for back up," he added while tapping the Glock 19.

Sparks continued. "Chopper's gonna be your main piece. You hold that trigger down and it's hot. We take Piety to Florida Avenue, go behind the action. Park there. Walk real quiet to Law and creep up to the building. After I take out the trooper guarding the entrance…"

"State trooper?!" warbled Grange. "You didn't tell me about shooting a trooper."

"Don't matter if I did. Tellin' you now." He said as an aside, "Gotdamn if I ain't gotta force-feed this baby."

"That's not fair," mumbled Grange. He felt his cheek. The pain of his bruise was throbbing.

"You listenin'? There's a second guard on Desire. Minute he hears his partner shot he's comin' 'round the corner. You gonna be waitin' for him. Cut him down," said Sparks.

"But that sounds bloody."

"Is what it is. I'll be inside takin' care-a them punks who kidnapped me. After you get the guard, you come inside and back me up. You know what I look like. Do not shoot me in the ass. Hear me?"

Grange nodded.

"Probably be a handful-a ninja lookin' dudes and the boss in a suit and tie. Maybe not the boss, maybe just the one the boss trusts, but he'll do. We don't leave 'til all-a them on the floor," emphasized Sparks.

"What about the men in cages you were telling me about?"

asked Grange. His words weren't yet on solid ground, more like the attempted flight of a bird with a damaged wing.

"What about 'em? Them brothers done nothin' to me. We ain't killin' 'em. Just the ninjas and Mr. Businessman. That's who we gunnin' for," misunderstood Sparks.

"Noooo," said Grange. The stretched out word was a roller coaster zipping downhill. "Leon, aren't we going to rescue them?"

Sparks looked at Grange like he'd laid an egg and was growing feathers. Pointed at the huddled man. Saw his own finger, considered it, and used it to pick his nose. Wiped it on the wall behind him.

"Rescue? What I look like, the Red Cross? You kiddin'? Them niggas been caged up who knows how long. Minute they get out they wantin' somebody to pay for their misery. Can't hate on that but ain't gonna be me. They come at me, I gotta kill all-a them on top-a all the others. That's 'bout thirty men, Morris. Nah, best thing for us and them is leave 'em be. Don't worry. Commotion we make is gonna draw a crowd. Once we shoot who we gotta shoot, we get out to the car, take off. Throw the guns in one-a the tall weed lots. Got it?"

"Guess so, but I don't see why…" said Grange.

"Come on now. Don't start," cautioned Sparks. "Look, Morris, no half-steppin' tonight. When we get back here, you do whatever you wanna do. Get lit. Think I care? I won't see you no more after today. Sure you won't mind that. But one thing."

"What is it, Leon?" asked Grange.

"After tonight you forget my name and all-a this. Hear me? My name don't come outta your mouth again. Let's practice. What's my name?"

"Huh? It's Le…oh, I, I haven't the foggiest idea."

Sparks got louder. "I said tell me my damn name. Now."

"I don't know, " replied Grange, sounding like an engine that couldn't quite start.

"My name! Say it!" yelled Sparks.

"Never heard it before!" screeched Grange.

Sparks nodded slowly as if his head was heavy, wrapped his arms around his belly, and let the faintest glimmer of a smile appear.

"Alright," he said.

Another conversation was taking place a few doors from the Law and Desire corner. It was between family and by phone.

"Mama, why don't you let it be?"

"Don't you get exasperated with me, Armand. You're in Philly. I'm here, knee-deep in it," said Sylvia Asbury.

Her son sighed. He'd been plucked from his FEMA trailer after Katrina to work for a foundation. His job was to decide how to wisely use the millions that various pro athletes put toward philanthropy. His mama had gotten him the job but regretted the distance ever since.

"I don't want to see you get hurt. That's all," said Armand.

"Don't give me pity, boy. Your mama was here when this was a thriving community, here when it was too hot, and gonna be here whatever it is in the future. I could deal with Franklin Glapion, right?"

"Franklin's was a mess," mused Armand.

"A lot of bar owners do the same thing, control the dealing so they keep the profits in house. That bar was low down, though," said Sylvia, referring to one of the few remaining structures in the block of Desire between Law and the Florida Canal.

The bar, cinderblock painted blue with cheerful wine glasses dancing on the front next to the name, had gone through a few incarnations. Only by change in ownership. No matter who was running things, it wasn't a bar for law abiding people.

Franklin Glapion was the owner and controlling drugs in that area, despite pushback from Sylvia, until the bar got flooded to the single story roof in 2005. He was uninsured, which didn't really matter since monthly premiums paid meant little when insurance companies were faced with actually holding up their end of the bargain after Katrina.

Glapion decided to torch the bar and collect that way. It would've worked, like it did for several others, except for a Black Hawk helicopter flying overhead, as they regularly were after the flood. Glapion was caught in the act of pouring gasoline on the façade, saw the helicopter seeing him, and decided to shoot it out of the sky.

Instead, he was the one shot down, and the bar sat vacant three doors down from the former Club Desire.

"It sure was low down," said Armand. He remembered all too well coming up in the blood-soaked 90's. Bodies piling up on bodies every day back then.

Sylvia went right back to the topic of disagreement. "I'm telling you, I left a message for Councilman Russell. Told him this none-a my business attitude from him was unacceptable. Why they need state troopers there? I didn't mention it, but I'm getting in there tonight."

"Mama," warned Armand.

"I am getting *in there* tonight," repeated Sylvia.

"Come on, now."

"Hear me? Getting in there *tonight*," she said.

"You don't even have a gun. Wait. Mama, you get a gun?" worried Armand.

"Please. I don't need no piece. I got peace in my heart, Armand. I'm armed, yes indeed. Armed with peace and the tenacity of a junkyard dog,"

"Damn, mama. You sound cold blooded."

"Son, I'm sick and tired. Something's going on in that club

that's not right. I can feel it."

She paused and in a calm manner said, "Tonight the bullshit ass lies disappear. I'm brewing a pot of coffee right now to help keep me up. Son, can you blame me?"

"No, you just worry me, that's all. Going up in there by yourself," he said

"What I'm gonna do, boy? Your sister's back in Baton Rouge. Most-a my neighbors are retired. Have old Mr. Parker come with me?" asked Sylvia.

"Oh my goodness," laughed Armand. "Picture him strollin' up to the state po-lice, moustache only on the left side, all long and waxed up. Flippin' those striped suspenders. Tappin' his toes together in the cowboy boots he painted. They probably fall over laughin', so you walk right in."

"Armand," chided Sylvia. "Herbie Parker is a little eccentric. Been that way his whole life."

"A little eccentric? Mama, every day. *Every day*," said Armand.

"I know. That's what he likes."

"Every day Mr. Parker gets on the Desire bus. Rides it past Canal. Walks to Tulane and Loyola. Takes the bus up Airline Highway to the airport for lunch. Then all that in reverse to get home. Every day."

"He's got his routine. Likes that Dooky Chase airport restaurant," said Sylvia.

"He sure does like Dooky Chase," laughed Armand.

"Man knows what he likes," said Sylvia. "Plus, I suspect he wants to see all the people coming and going. You're in Philly. He's never been anywhere north of Baton Rouge. Anyway, speaking of coming and going, in a few hours I'm most definitely finding out what's going on in that old Club Desire."

Chapter 14

At 9:37 p.m. Monday night, two men dressed in black were preparing inside a Mid City produce warehouse. The one with an oversized head had opened the back doors of a white van. He was pressing buttons on the inside of each door to make sure the automatic windows were working.

"Frankie, whatta we need that for? Tonight's just transportation, right? Load 'em, lock 'em in, take a little drive, and unload 'em," said the younger man walking toward the van with a rug under his arm.

"I'm fuckin' aware of the job, but you never know how things could change. Coverin' our tails is what I'm doin'. Okay, Ray?"

"We're not takin' my sniper chair, are we? All those punks'd be fightin' over who gets the big seat for the ride," said Ray.

Frankie looked to his right at the wooden chair mounted on the end of two 2x4's. When they were on hit missions, they'd load up the structure in the back of the van. Frankie drove. Always.

Ray would sit in the back on the chair so he could see out one of the rear windows. When their target was directly behind them, Ray would lower the windows, usually the one on the right. He'd quickly place the barrel of his AK-47 out the window and shoot the person who needed to get got.

Frankie sighed, remembering his days of running the Lucky Lake riverboat casino in the 90's. "Don't be stupid," he said. "The chair stays here. You just make sure the rifle's in your possession. Get it out of the back the second we arrive there."

"You don't have to worry, Frankie," said Ray. "Why the hell we movin' the criminals anyway? Where to?"

"Dunno yet, Ray. Somewhere across the Claiborne Bridge

in the Lower Ninth Ward."

Ray paused from unrolling the rug on the cement floor and looked up.

"You gotta be kiddin'. Sendin' us down to the goddamn C.T.C.," he said.

"Stop makin' shit up. C.T.C. means nothin'," scoffed Frankie.

"Course I know what it means. Cut Throat City. You've never heard that before, old man," mocked Ray.

Frankie closed the van doors firmly with hands that were over twenty years older than Ray's fifty-odd years. The window testing was complete.

"No, I never heard that because the only time I go there I'm in a fuckin' hurry to get through that shit and end up at Rocky and Carlo's," he said in a ridiculing way.

"You think I hang out there. No, Frankie. I hear things."

"Do I look like I give a fuck, Ray?" Frankie ran his hands through his thinning hair and checked his watch. "Come on, already. We gotta be there at 10. That's twenty minutes from now."

"Give me a break," muttered Ray. He checked the gun, made sure he had plenty of ammo, and rerolled it all up in the small rug. He opened the back doors of the van, quietly cursing that Frankie had closed them, and placed the fabric cylinder inside.

Shortly after, they left the warehouse onto Maurepas, Ray closed and locked the garage door, and Frankie drove off. He made a loop to follow the one-way streets around, taking Lapeyrouse a few blocks before turning left onto Broad.

They'd barely begun to drive downriver when a tall thin fellow on a bike with a rigged-up motor saw them pass by while he idled at Onzaga and Broad. Though it was night and plenty dark, the bicyclist Window could see the passengers of the sought after white van looked like rough guys. He called it in to his leader Nat in a froggy voice while he turned right and followed after.

Window kept a steady distance back from the van. He wasn't trained in matters of surveillance, but with the motor engaged his maximum speed was 25 mph. His concoction of pasta, hydrogen peroxide, and yeast from beard clippings powered the motor that putt-putted slow enough for him to keep an eye on the van and for them not to know it.

"Nat, we're at St. Bernard now" and "Heading up Elysian Fields toward the lake" were a few of his updates, upon which the bike gang leader in turn notified the rest of the group. They began to slowly swarm toward Window's moving location. None of the other bicycles were motorized, so it took time.

His final update was whispered. "Window to Nat. I cut my motor so they couldn't hear me. The van's parked in front of a large abandoned building at the intersection of Law and Desire. I suspect it's their stash house for stolen bikes. I'm a few doors from them. Along the side of a house. It's really dark."

Window was all business. The time on his phone was 10:06 p.m.

Parked in front of the van was an SUV with Councilman Rob Russell inside, waiting for the scene to unveil itself. Russell's face was uncovered, defying the request. His Chief of Staff Kevin Warren was directing things inside the club to Frankie, Ray, two state troopers, and a few off duty NOPD officers. Kevin and the troopers were the only ones of the crew not dressed entirely in black. All had their faces covered with masks.

"Before each one goes from his holding cell into the back of the van, make sure his blindfold and gag are tight. Take off his shoes too. Throw them into the middle of the floor. Less chance he tries to make a run for it," instructed Kevin. He spoke softly enough so as not to be heard by those in the cages.

"All the prisoners will be transported by van to the new site. Follow me there. They'll be unloaded. Troopers will hold them while the rest of you come back here. The U-Haul truck should arrive by then, and you'll load up the holding cells and transport them to the new site. It may take a few trips. Got it?"

Meanwhile outside, Window was prone and looking kitty corner at the building. He'd stashed his bike under the house and was nestled alongside it.

He saw the indoor lights turn off directly across the street and heard the front door barely creak open. Made himself as flat as possible but kept his chin up enough to be able to see.

Window could barely make out a person, probably a woman, exiting the house and softly closing the door. She crept lightly down her steps, snuck across the yard, and turned left onto the sidewalk toward the club and the white van.

The lens of Window's gaze followed her and also ahead of her, seeing for the first time another vehicle. It was parked in front of the van. If there were more he couldn't tell from his angle.

"A bunch of people are in on this. Who knows how many stolen bikes are in that big blighted building. This isn't a couple crackheads. It's a conspiracy," he murmured by phone to Nat who assured him the U-Lock Bike Gang was on their way.

When the woman reached the corner, she was out in the open, right next to the street signs indicating Law and Desire. She'd pushed the city to put them up in 2006 but had been unsuccessful in getting the broken streetlights fixed. Weekly calls to the 311 information and complaint line were as fruitless as griping to her councilman.

It struck her as ironic that the cover of night was to her benefit. "Who'd have thought?" mused Sylvia Asbury.

"No guard on the Desire side. First time I haven't seen anyone there. Can't see yet on the Law side what with the van blocking my view," she said to herself.

Sylvia squatted down as far as she could without hurting her back, leaned forward, and crept across the street.

She saw four parked vehicles. The SUV and the van were the closest two. She tip toed quickly. First the van. Next the SUV.

Her nostrils flared and she fell to the ground with surprise. She was on her hands and knees, mouth wide open and gaping down to the street.

"The councilman's here. Rob Russell's a part of all this. I'll be," she said. He was in the passenger seat, waiting on whoever was inside.

Sylvia kept to all fours and crawled between the two vehicles, which put her directly in line with the entrance surrounded by glass cubes that used to light up in the old days and welcome patrons to the ticket booth on the left.

Gravel, broken glass, and who knows what else cut into her flesh as she crawled toward the entrance hoping Russell wouldn't see her. She heard the murmur of voices inside as she made it to the entranceway.

"I see flashlights and a few people but can't tell what's going on," she said to herself. "Other than a guy wearing a suit and tie with tan loafers who looks in charge."

Sylvia went a little further, not inside but far enough to widen her view. What she saw astonished her.

Black men were being removed from small cages at gunpoint by state troopers and other men. A couple prisoners were sitting on the floor taking their shoes off. All of them, the prisoners and their captors, had their faces obscured, either by blindfolds or masks. The only person she could recognize was Rob Russell inside the SUV near her.

"I'll be damned. Turned that old club into an off-the-books prison. No wonder Rob was blowin' off my calls. No wonder nobody else wanted to talk about this place. 'Calm down, Sylvia. Mountain out of a molehill, Sylvia,' they said. Mmm hmm. I'm not gonna stop 'til Councilman Russell's corrupt dirty self is locked up."

She crawled backward a bit, turned, and scurried between the two vehicles. "Need a minute to think. Who can I call?" she wondered.

Bobby Delery automatically looked over from his TV to the clock when the landline phone rang. 10:17. Later than usual for a call. Maybe it was her. He paused the movie playing, which froze Donnie Yen midway through a jumping kick.

"Hello," he answered.

"No 'Delery residence' answer, huh?" the voice responded.

"I'm just tired. Not feeling very formal," he said. Delery was glad it was her.

"I'm only teasing," said Ellis. "Sorry it's later than usual. Family dinner. The wine was flowing. Vonetta's on spring break."

"Spring break in April," he said absentmindedly.

"You do sound tired, Bobby. LSU's late for some reason. You were going to try and meet with a few people. Any updates?"

Delery filled her in generally and added, "I don't know if this has anything to do with it, but I've been going over the words Isaac and Curtis were trying to pass on."

"Like a code? What are they?" she asked.

"Desire. Saw him at the club. Law |. The symbol after Law is a line, like a lower-case letter "L," know what I mean?"

"I'm following," said Ellis. "Repeat it again. I assume the order doesn't matter."

"No, that's reverse order how I got the information, but it doesn't matter anyway," he clarified.

"Let's see," she said, letting the words loop in her mind. "The symbol's got me wondering. What do you think it stands for?"

"I don't know," admitted Delery. "Isaac was writing it as he was dying. Maybe he didn't finish what he wanted to say."

"That makes it tricky. Over half of the alphabet starts that way." She repeated it all aloud. "Desire. Law |. Saw him at the club. Law |. Desire. Saw him at the club. Hmm."

"You have an idea?" he asked.

"This is probably silly, but were the "D" in Desire and "L" in Law capitalized?"

"According to what I read and was told," Delery confirmed.

"Okay," Ellis said. "Reason I ask is growing up one of my neighbors was an old man named Wilton Perkins. He's passed on now, but when I was a kid he'd tell me stories about playing music decades before. Said he was a drummer for some household names. Haven't thought about all that in years, but he did say there was a big deal place called Club Desire. I remember his face when he told me it was at Law and Desire. He said, 'Can't make up anything outlandish enough to beat the street names.' What do you think?"

"I don't know," said Delery. "That part of the Ninth Ward must've flooded real bad. Is there anything open back there, especially a music club?"

"I doubt it. Told you it was silly. Are we still going to the gym tomorrow morning?"

They made their Tuesday plans and concluded the call.

Delery remembered his mama telling him, "Don't you go wandering on foot, Bobby. If you're on somebody else's turf, they will whup you. Especially if you go across the Florida Canal."

He'd never been in the area Ellis was talking about, but insomnia would keep him up anyway. "It's a straight shot to take Desire from the river and keep going all the way back," he thought.

Maybe she'd nailed it. Isaac was about to make the '+' sign when he died, and it all fit together at one intersection.

"Nah, it's too much of a long shot. But it's not even 10:30 yet. I drive there and back, be home by 11:00," he said.

In all his years, he'd never wanted a gun, but on a Monday night in April he wished he had one.

While Delery made the drive, Sylvia Asbury stood at the sidewalk in front of her house. View was limited, but she could see activity around the club as men were slowly loaded into the back of the van.

Window stayed under the house across the street so she couldn't see him, which also meant he was no witness to the load in of the shoeless prisoners. Figured he hide there until the bike gang arrived.

Sylvia whispered into her phone, "There's a fire in the 2600 block of Desire. At the corner. Get the trucks out here. Houses on either side might go up too. Babies inside." She was pushing certain buttons to get first responders out immediately. It was an old New Orleans trick. Might wait on NOPD for hours, but make it sound like an NOFD matter and get a quick response.

In the situation at hand she was also using the ploy because of not knowing which police in the 5th District she could trust.

"Oh no," Sylvia said a little louder when she heard the van doors close along with those of the other vehicles. They were all about to leave. She hurried to the corner, not minding anymore if they saw her. Would the firemen show up soon?

Headlights illuminated the night, providing enough light that she hunched behind the sign post too thin to provide any cover. Window crawled out from his space and watched her.

Suddenly a vehicle thundered at a fast clip from the left on Law. Leon Sparks and Morris Grange were approaching with the realization they were about to miss their targets. Sparks, seeing the headlights, abandoned their plan to sneak around from the side and instead sped directly toward the sources of the lights.

He yelled, "Morris, roll your window down! Grab the big gun, lean out, and start shooting!"

Grange was unaccustomed to firing any sort of weapon, particularly when in a speeding BMW. As Sparks got them half a block away, Grange pushed down on the safety lever with his thumb as previously instructed and turned his body so his left hand could support the dominant right which held the loaded AK-47.

"Fire, Morris, fire!" pushed Sparks.

Grange was nervous and tired, though that didn't change the result much. Before the kick of the recoil proved too much for him and he dropped the gun onto his lap, he mostly sprayed the sky, street, and surrounding weeds. Two bullets found their mark, not a human one but still effective.

Kevin Warren had edged his SUV out of its place as the third of the four car caravan so they could lead. Both men ducked when they heard the bullets skipping along the street. The next sound was a loud "Poosh." Not an airbag inflating but the left front tire deflating.

"Kevin, let's go inside the club. Quickly," urged Russell as he scurried out the passenger side. They darted inside, dodged cages, and the pile of almost two dozen sneakers on their way across the large room to the rickety stairs on the far side. Raced for their lives up to the second floor, jumped into the first room they saw, and closed the door.

Outside the club, Sparks and Grange were still approaching, but the sound of ¾ of a magazine thrashing around was gone. The cuffed prisoners inside the back of the van were huddled and strewn atop each other in fear. Frankie in the driver's seat poked his head up, saw the SUV approaching, and broke from the plan by hurtling the van from its spot.

Sparks was in the middle of the road, where he'd pulled to give Grange a better angle for shooting. "Gotdamn if you didn't fuck it all up!" he shouted while reaching in the backseat for another weapon.

"Leon, look out!" called Grange as the van sped toward them. Driving one-handed, Sparks cranked the wheel to the right, taking them into a pile of tires and abandoned trailer next to a boarded-up house.

The van careened past, filling the space where the BMW had been. The other two vehicles came to life and followed the van. Sparks struggled for a bit before reversing and heading back the way he'd driven in so he could chase them.

Sparks sighed, scratched the outer ring of his left nostril with a free hand, and recalled his father telling him that the scratchy nose was a genetic trait passed down from Leon's great-great-great-great grandfather who was owned by a corrosive-minded man named Ezekiel Sparks.

The only sound Sylvia could hear shortly after from her spot on the ground was the pulsing beat of her heart. She'd dropped there upon the arrival of gunfire. "Where are the firemen?"

She stood up, dusted herself off, and looked over. Only car still there was tilted to the side on a flat tire. The empty SUV Rob Russell had been sitting in. Sylvia walked over to it. "They're inside," she said, having seen them dash into the club and hoping NOFD would show soon.

As Sylvia walked back to her house, she first heard a murmuring of voices followed by the physical presence of a bicycle cluster heading her way. She was further startled by Window running from across the street to meet them.

"It's the building on the corner," Window said in a proud bass. "That's the bike stash house. A shootout just went down, but the white van and everybody else drove off. Must be a bunch of bikes in there."

"Yes!" praised bike gang leader Nat. He followed that with a jumping high five that about dislocated Window's arm. "Fuck yeah. Good work, Window. This is where the crackheads have been keepin' 'em, huh?"

Sylvia walked into the street. She'd had no choice but to overhear them. "Actually, men were caged inside. There weren't any bikes there."

The U-Lock Bike Gang ignored her as they all walked their wheels to the club. "It's a big place," said Nat. "Can you imagine how many bikes are in there?"

Sylvia tried once again. "There were people locked up inside, not...oh, forget it."

The bicyclists marched to the corner, crossed the street, and angled over to the club's entrance. Nat appointed two of them to stay outside and guard all the wheels.

Councilman Rob Russell and Kevin Warren quietly eased open the door, thinking enough time had passed after the gunshots. Just as suddenly they heard voices on the first floor, so they darted back into the room. Warren gently pulled the door closed.

"Holy shit," said Nat in awe as if viewing the Roman Colosseum. "These are some smart junkies. Lock up the stolen bikes in cages until they sell, so squatters won't grab 'em. It's the stash house of all stash houses. The junkies have outdone themselves. Must be a new breed."

Nat and the rest of the brigade gathered inside looked around speechlessly. Window walked over to Nat and whispered in his ear. Nat nodded and patted Window on the back.

"Okay, comrades. We've met our enemy. Crackhead 2.0. We were too late to catch 'em this time, but they can't store the bikes if the stash house is gone," said Nat.

He walked over to the pile of sneakers, shoes that retailed for $100-500, took a lighter from his pocket with his right hand, and gestured with his other for the rest to join him.

"ULBG don't mess around," Nat began chanting. He continued keeping the flame going until a pair of futuristic looking Nike's with red leather uppers, white rubber lowers, and red laces started to burn. All around him, the rest of the bike gang started doing the same, chanting and burning shoes.

Window realized another step was necessary, so he grabbed a stray piece of wood and used it to push the fiery shoes off to the side next to wooden support posts. The smoke from the leather, rubber, suede, and more exotic materials began to make the bike gang cough, so they ran out, grabbed their respective steeds, and wheeled off into the night.

Chapter 15

The U-Lockers passed Bobby Delery who was standing with Sylvia. He'd arrived on the scene while the bike gang was inside the club.

"They're in a hurry," said Delery.

"Pssh. Didn't find what they were looking for. There weren't stolen bikes in there, only stolen people. 'Course they don't care about that. But I know what I saw," said Sylvia.

Delery studied her for a moment, not knowing for sure if he'd uncovered a sinister situation or she was full-on nuts. He turned his head toward the club. She did too and both of them sniffed.

"Burning tires?" wondered Delery.

"I don't know, but look," pointed Sylvia. "Good thing the firemen are on the way."

"How would you know to call them before…" he started.

"Oh my goodness!" Sylvia realized. "He's gonna make me look like a chump. Burning all the evidence and the club with it. That's what he's doing in there," she said while running as quickly as she could the few hundred feet to the Club Desire entrance.

Delery followed. "Who are you talking about?" he asked. Remembering to throw out his wild card, "Does he have a white van?"

Sylvia didn't break stride. "They took men out of cages and loaded them all up in a white van."

This was unexpected information to Delery. Sounded completely different than how his brothers died. But yet, maybe it was connected.

"Who's burning the evidence?" he asked.

They both reached the entrance. The smell was much worse. "Councilman Russell. He's the one behind the whole mess. Saw him outside supervising it all," she said.

"Rob Russell. *The* Rob Russell? Kidnapping people?" wondered Delery, but Sylvia was ducking inside.

"Look at this," she said, but Delery already saw it. A room filled with human-sized cages. Both covered their noses and mouths. The recessed area under the second floor balcony and rooms was filling up with flames. The lone staircase collapsed.

In response, one of the second floor doors flung open. Two jumped out coughing. Their eyes filled with terror when they caught sight of the fire.

"Oh, shit!" exclaimed Rob Russell. He and Kevin Warren were trapped on the second floor, and the smoke from the burning sneakers was getting more acrid by the moment.

Russell pictured himself on a boat cruising around Lake Pontchartrain. Saw he was wearing his favorite pinstriped shirt, buttoned all the way to the end of his wrists and crisply tucked into a pair of pleated shorts. Deck shoes on his feet. Never again unless he got out quickly.

Each pair saw the other. "Ms. Asbury, you've got to help us," called out Russell. Warren seconded it. "Please get us down from here."

The smoke was getting too toxic for Delery and Sylvia.

"Did you have anything to do with the deaths of my brothers Isaac and Curtis Delery?" asked Delery, rushing his words.

"There's no time for any of that," said Russell. "Get me out of here, and we'll find out who did it."

Sylvia turned to Delery. "He killed your family?"

"Ask him," said Delery.

"We were only making the city safer," said Warren. He was frantic. "That's all. Help us."

The flames crept up the support posts like expanding

plumage, inching closer to the second floor. The crackling sound was suddenly outmatched by an approaching fire engine.

"Thank goodness. Let them know we're in here," pleaded Russell.

"This smoke is too much for me," coughed Sylvia. She pointed up at the two. "Better start praying." She turned and left.

Delery narrowed his eyes. "I'm gonna ask you again. Were you…"

"Yes, yes," blurted out Warren. "It was wrong, but it wasn't my decision. It was his. The whole plan. Even spreading the rumors your brother was a snitch." He pointed at Russell. "Help me, please. Don't let me die because of him."

"You coward," sneered Russell.

All three men started coughing as the smoke began to take over the space and filled the air.

"I'm leaving now," said Delery. His nostrils were beginning to fill up. He pointed at Russell and Warren. "I can live with you two going down." Their desperate yelling didn't sway him. Even the building wanted them dead.

Delery ran outside and took in gulping amounts of air.

Sylvia was standing at the corner as NOFD Engine #8 rolled up. Delery rushed up to her. Russell and Warren couldn't be heard from that distance.

"Anyone inside?" asked the first fireman off the truck.

"No, no one," Delery immediately responded. "I was just in there checking. Didn't see a soul."

"No one inside. Looks like it was arson," Sylvia added. Remembering what she'd seen earlier, she said, "I think they used a bunch of shoes to torch it."

"That explains the type of smoke," said the captain who'd joined them as a ladder truck, rescue unit, and another engine truck pulled up. "Can't send my guys inside. It's too hazardous.

No babies in there, huh? 911 got it wrong again."

He turned and instructed his men to attack the fire from the exterior. Delery and Sylvia walked away from the harsh smoke that was beginning to permeate the outside.

She shook her head. "There's so much that could've been done with that old club. If fire can't take it down, the city will. All that history. But if it's going down, who better to go down with it?"

"Agreed," said Delery. "If I'd had time to really think over that decision, I'm not sure I'd walk away. Spur of the moment, though, man's gotta do what he's gotta do. Or not do."

They introduced themselves and Sylvia invited him over for dinner the following night.

"No talking about what we saw in there. Rob Russell and the other one. The fire department will find their bodies or somebody'll match up the SUV," she said.

"Don't worry," he assured. "It's our secret. Would you think I was too rude if I wanted to bring one or two people with me?"

She beamed. "'Course not. The more the merrier. Bring yourselves and something to drink."

Tuesday, the next evening, saw four people gathered around Sylvia's dining room table.

"Last night was an active one. Of course the big fire a few doors down. The drownings too," said Detective Nelson Harrell.

"Now, detective. Death and destruction talk at dinner," scolded Sylvia. "Will you pass the beans, please?" she asked, gesturing toward a baking dish.

"Two cars tried to go over the Claiborne Bridge while the drawbridge was rising. I realize the state troopers aren't from here, but still. Sorry, ma'am," said Ellis Smith.

"I guess if it's as common as the sun rising, why not talk about it? And call me Sylvia, my baby."

Bobby Delery had largely been a man of few words at the table. Though he'd invited Harrell, he wanted to be cautious of slipping and saying anything the Homicide Detective might pick up on. Delery also realized he'd been too quiet. That was equally suspicious.

"From what I read, the state police were seen in the midst of four vehicles by the bridge operator. Only the last two cars didn't make it over in time. Troopers and a used car dealer with a passenger and some guns," said Delery, leaving out that a white van had been seen in front of the pack. He was confused how all of it fit together but wasn't about to begin speculating aloud.

Sylvia acted like she was consumed with spooning out a portion of green beans but was in fact listening intently. If necessary, she'd cut him off.

"A white van again," said Harrell, filling in the blank while looking at Delery. "Question is why the troopers were chasing it and the car dealer was behind them? And why they hadn't called it in? Odd also that it happened only a few minutes after the fire."

Harrell surveyed the group before glancing down to stab a piece of baked fish with his fork.

"I don't know about all that with the bridge. I was here. It's been a tough day," said Sylvia.

"The fire, of course," said Ellis.

"There's more to it that hasn't made the papers yet," started Sylvia.

Delery's stomach turned. He forced himself to project a happy-go-lucky smile laced with sadness.

Sylvia continued. "I was the one who called 911 the minute I smelled smoke. It was a harsh kind. There was an SUV next to the club, but since it had a flat, I just figured it was abandoned. Happens back here. Kids steal a car and joyride long as they can. I would never have guessed it was the councilman's car."

She had the room in her palm, so she kept unraveling the ball of string.

"Bobby was stopping by to visit. How long we known each other?"

Delery quickly inserted himself. "Oh, only six months. Remember, I've been in Chicago."

Sylvia nodded a little too heartily. "That's right. Only six months. How time flies. So, Bobby got here after I called 911, and I had him go in the old Club Desire with me to make sure no one was in there. We didn't see anyone."

"Didn't hear anyone either," added Delery, understanding what she was doing.

"We couldn't stay inside very long. The inspector said someone had lit a bunch of sneakers to start the fire. That's why the smoke was so bad. Toxic," said Sylvia.

"Is that why you've been so quiet? Earlier and tonight?" Ellis asked Delery.

He nodded. "There was no sign of anyone in there. If we'd known, maybe we could've saved them."

"I feel like it's my fault," said Sylvia. "I'd been leaning on the councilman to develop the club for a community center. He must've come by to check it out, and look what happened to him and his Chief of Staff."

"Here's what's strange, though," said Harrell. He'd been sitting back taking it all in.

"I think it's safe to say Rob Russell wasn't the arsonist. Devil's advocate—if he was he'd have left immediately. Why would an arsonist go in after Russell and his head guy were there, torch the place, and them not know about it to get out?"

Delery jumped on that. "My guess would be that somebody followed them in, killed them, and started the fire to cover it up."

"Maybe, except I'll divulge what I heard earlier. The coroner's showing cause of death as smoke inhalation. What about the cages?" asked Harrell.

"The what?" wondered Sylvia innocently.

"You two were in there, weren't you? You had to have seen holding cells. If I didn't know better I'd think unlawful detention was going on. Don't get me wrong. I'm not accusing the councilman of anything. This is all off the record. We're just talking."

Sylvia angled her eyebrows and pursed her lips. "I don't know what those were for. Of course we saw them, but our immediate concern was that a person or animal needed rescuing. There certainly was no one in the cages when we went inside."

One thing didn't sit well with Ellis. She was the one who'd tipped Delery off about the intersection, yet he somehow knew Sylvia.

"How did the two of you meet?" Ellis asked, looking first at Sylvia to her left and Delery straight across.

"A community event," said Delery as Sylvia said, "A second line."

Delery shrugged. "At a second line going to an event at the Marsalis Center. In Musician's Village."

He saw Ellis looking at him in a peculiar way, so he expanded on his response. It had clicked in his mind where the questioning was going.

"We had such a nice chat, exchanged numbers. What's it been, Sylvia, a couple times we got together for lunch?"

Sylvia wasn't sure where he was going, but she nodded.

Delery continued, but he didn't want to mention the connection of "Law |," "Desire," and "Saw him at the club" in front of Harrell.

He started off, "So, when Sylvia called and asked me to rush over, I knew I'd never been in that particular part of the Upper

Ninth."

Next he pivoted, "I had no idea the history back here. It's sad that not only did the building burn down, but the city's got to remove the slab too. Asbestos, Sylvia?"

She took the baton and kept going, regaling the others about how her family's history and that of the stretch of Desire were linked. Mentioned the musical acts that played Club Desire. That there'd been a salon, medical center, meat market, supermarket, hardware store, and more in addition to all the music in the block. About some of the characters like Polkadot Slim who ran a club named after him. And her frustration that so much media attention was focused on the Lower Ninth Ward while those in the Florida Canal area of the Upper Ninth weren't given crumbs.

It was a power move by Delery, knowing that once Sylvia started she was a talker and superb teller of stretched stories like any true New Orleanian. Knowing that neither Harrell nor Ellis would interrupt to clear up questions or inconsistencies in the involvement of Sylvia and Delery with the previous night's events. And knowing that the sheer amount of information would help to obliterate any train of thought the detective might otherwise have about the fire, deaths, and drownings. All in all, what Delery had intended by inviting Ellis and Harrell.

An hour later, when the dinner guests stood on the porch of Sylvia's raised house, she gave each of them a hug.

"It's all gone," she said, looking across the intersection at a smoldering lot that hadn't sat empty for over sixty years.

"But it was so nice having you all over. Community. People. That's what keeps us going. And Bobby, you told me she was pretty. Hope you know how to treat a rare beauty."

"Sylvia," said an embarrassed Ellis.

"Listen here, my baby," said Sylvia. "Ashes to ashes. Dust to dust. But in the meantime, a lady's gotta represent. Am I wrong?"

She embraced each of them again, and Harrell accompanied Delery and Ellis down the sixteen steps. They paused at the bottom.

"Nice to meet you, Ellis. Thanks for the invite, Bobby."

They all shook hands and turned toward their respective cars.

"Heading home when we get back to my place?" Delery asked Ellis.

She stopped walking and whispered in his ear, "How about a real good place in about ten minutes?"

He put his arm around her. "You say that and I'll drive it in five."

Mayor Walter Vaccaro's grandfather clock chimed nine times in his Uptown home office. It was a replica of the one that sat in his family house for years. The original had been a gift from one of his father's unofficial business partners. A man named Carlos Marcello. He quietly ran the whole region decades before. So powerful that then-U.S. Attorney General Bobby Kennedy had him taken from the streets of New Orleans and dropped off in the Guatemalan jungle. Twice. The little big man had made his way back each time.

Vaccaro ran his left hand along the fine cherry wood of the clock. "Priscilla, good talkin' to you," he said in an old New Orleans accent more commonly heard outside of New Orleans. "However the council decides to honor Rob Russell, you've got the backing of my office."

His next call was to Percy Charbonnet who'd handled real estate for the Vaccaro family ever since Walter was a toddler.

"Hey Perce. It's Walter. Look, I wanna unload that produce warehouse at Maurepas and Crete. It's in my name only, so none-a my brothers or sisters need to cosign. Quickly, alright. Empty warehouse isn't doing anything for me. Make sure it's all in the LLC. Keep my name out of it. I've got enough shit to deal with. Some bozo might try to make hay of this too."

Vaccaro walked from his clock and closed the office door. He took another phone out of a locked desk drawer. Spoke a little softer but with no less emphasis.

"Frankie, look. You and Ray take care of the van? Gun too?"

"Sure thing. Chop shop under the Huey Long Bridge this morning. Gun's at the bottom of Bayou St. John."

Vaccaro's narrowed eyes looked a little less concerned.

"Good. My name never came out of Russell's stupid mouth, right?"

Frankie laughed. "Nah, dumbshit had no idea I've been workin' for the Vaccaro's for years. Definitely had no fuckin' idea where we stored the van."

"Yeah, about that. I'm selling the warehouse. Don't want any blowback on this. Can't have any way it can be connected to me. You and I know this was Russell's big money making plan, but how would I explain…"

"Don't worry," assured Frankie. "All loose ends were taken care of,"

"What's that mean, Frankie? You know what I have to ask you," cautioned Vaccaro with an edge in his voice.

"Don't worry about it," said Frankie vaguely.

"Goddamn it. I gotta be at a ribbon cutting for a new Central City pool tomorrow. Last thing I want is to be splashin' around with a bunch of kids and have this blow up in my face," hissed Vaccaro.

"Walter, Walter," soothed Frankie. "How long I been doin' this? Longevity comes from followin' orders and keepin' my fuckin' mouth shut. Crisis came up last night, I couldn't reach Russell by phone—now we know why—so I called you."

"Okay," said Vaccaro tentatively. "And?"

"We released 'em all out the back of the van like you said.

Told 'em they talked about what happened, they were dead. Used bolt cutters to take care of all the cuffs. It's all good, Walter. Nothin' but a fuckin' rainbow."

The carjackers who'd finally finished selling off the bikes they'd lucked upon inside another white van, the one stolen from Land of 1,000 Bikes, felt the same way.

Michael Allen Zell is a New Orleans-based novelist, essayist, and playwright. Zell's work has been published in *The Los Angeles Review of Books, Cerise Press, Disonare, Entrepot, Exquisite Corpse, NOLA Defender, Room 220,* and *Sleepingfish. Errata,* his first novel, was named a 'Top 10 Book of 2012' by *The Times-Picayune.* His first play, *What Do You Say To A Shadow?,* was named a 'Top 10 Play of the Year' in 2013 by *The Times-Picayune.* He has worked as a bookseller since 2001.

Lavender Ink
New Orleans
lavenderink.org

Made in the USA
Charleston, SC
18 October 2016